The Nine Lives of Doctor Who

The Nine Lives of Doctor Who

Peter Haining

23 November 1963 – a legend begins ...

HEADLINE

For Jeremy and Paula
They know why – or should it be Who?

First published in 1999
by HEADLINE BOOK PUBLISHING

10 9 8 7 6 5 4 3 2 1

British Library Cataloguing in Publication Data
    Haining, Peter. 1940-
    The nine lives of Doctor Who
    1. Doctor Who (Television program) 2. Doctor Who
    (Fictitious character)
    I. Title
    791.4'575

ISBN 0 7472 2243 6

Designed by Isobel Gillan
Typeset by Letterpart Limited, Reigate, Surrey
Printed and bound in Italy by Rotolito Lombarda SpA

HEADLINE BOOK PUBLISHING
A division of Hodder Headline PLC
338 Euston Road
London NW1 3BH

www.headline.co.uk
www.hodderheadline.com

Contents

The Man of Many Parts

? For a number of years I received letters from a fan of *Doctor Who* living in a remote little community in the Rocky Mountains of western Canada. His knowledge of the series was encyclopaedic and in his early correspondence he sought advice from me on certain facts about the programme which he thought I might be able to answer because of my association with it and the books I had written. There was nothing unusual in his first couple of letters to suggest he was any different from the dozens of other enthusiastic fans who have written to me through the years from all over the world. Then, in the third, he strongly disputed an answer I had given him, insisting he knew *better*. How? Because, he explained, *he* was a Time Lord and, like the Doctor, had come originally in a TARDIS from the planet Gallifrey.

I have met plenty of kinds of eccentricity in my years as a journalist, publisher and writer. But this was the first time I had been in contact with someone who believed they came from an imaginary world in a television science fiction series. His criticism was, in fact, about a statement Tom Baker's Doctor had made, I forget now exactly which. But, I had explained in my reply, Tom was an *actor* and what he was doing was speaking the lines he had been given. Any discrepancies were the fault of the writer, although I did stress that the people making *Doctor Who* always went to great pains to make sure inconsistencies were eliminated as much as was humanly possible. Well, my letter writer from his lofty heights in the Rockies exclaimed, he *knew* and insisted that I put the Doctor right. I am afraid my reply was brief and to the point. I reiterated that it was only a story and I was sorry he could not accept my explanation – but those *were* the facts. And as I wrote I was reminded of something amusing that Terry Nation, creator of the Daleks – who received a far larger postbag than mine – had once said when replying to anomalies of plot that had been pointed out to him by viewers: 'I think you must be forgetting the secret formula X divided by 375 multiplied by 279, which I'm sure you'll agree overcomes your objection fully.'

I received several more letters after that – to which I did not reply – in very much the same vein. In truth, they rather saddened me to think that someone had become so obsessed with what was, after all, an entertainment; that it had taken over his life, literally and figuratively. But it did bring home to me once again the amazing influence television, and its most popular shows in particular, can have on the minds and imaginations of viewers. To my correspondent, each of the actors playing the Doctor had no life beyond that. No family, no friends, not even a career beyond the boundaries of *Doctor Who*. So if there is one underlying purpose to this book, it is to show that the nine men who have portrayed the Doctor have had lives before and after the series. In truth, I might well have called the book *The Eighteen Lives of Doctor Who*, because all are fascinating people in their quite different ways and have achieved a great deal outside the programme. Now that 35 years have passed since the series was launched in November 1963 – marked in November 1998 by '35 Up' at BAFTA – what better moment to celebrate their achievements?

For the purists, I should perhaps just make it clear that Peter Cushing, the second man to play the Doctor, is generally considered a 'rogue Doctor' and not included with the eight TV actors because he did not regenerate from his predecessor, nor pass on the role to the next actor in line. Cushing, who played the part before William Hartnell relinquished it to Patrick Troughton, did, though, I believe, contribute significantly to the success of the legend of *Doctor Who* and deserves a place in this book. In the event, his two movies have subsequently proved to be the forerunners of the most recent Doctor, Paul McGann's adventure, namely *Doctor Who – The Movie*.

Doctor Who started out as a family-orientated programme with what was feared might be a limited life-span. Instead it became an international success attracting over one hundred million viewers around the world at its peak and now has a cult following despite not having been made as a series for more than a decade. The story of its genesis has been told many times. It is, though, I feel important to recap the major behind-the-scenes incidents of this astonishing story for the benefit of the latest generation of viewers who have discovered the time-travelling Doctor only through the re-runs of his adventures. Not to mention taking the opportunity of adding some new facts and opinions that have come to light with the benefit of hindsight for the interest of long-time admirers of the series.

The first episode of *Doctor Who*, 'An Unearthly Child' was screened at 5.25 p.m. on Saturday, 23 November 1963 after saturation coverage during the preceding twenty-four hours of the assassination of President Kennedy in Dallas, Texas. Like most people of my generation I can remember exactly what I was doing when news of the death of the charismatic young American leader was broken on radio and television – I was driving from my job as a newspaper reporter in Essex to the family home in Surrey. It was a numbing piece of news and one that was difficult to take in at first.

William Hartnell, the first Doctor, on the TARDIS set with co-star William Russell.

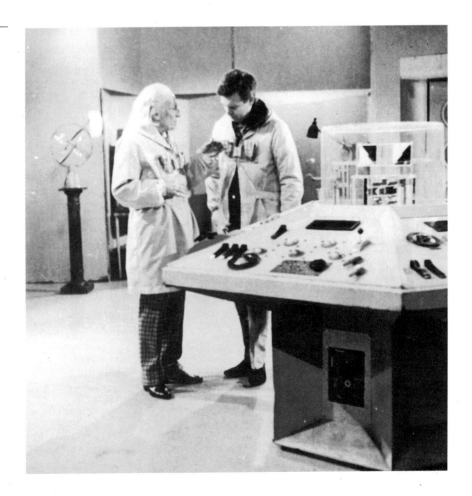

The 'rogue' Doctor,
Peter Cushing, with
co-stars Jennie Linden
(rear) and Roberta
Tovey.

Radio and television schedules were, not surprisingly, jettisoned as the world tried to absorb the terrible news coming from America. It was not until the Saturday evening, in fact, that BBC TV announcers told the nation that the normal evening's programmes would recommence shortly after 5 p.m. with the pop record show, *Juke Box Jury*, hosted by David Jacobs; the legendary police series, *Dixon of Dock Green* starring Jack Warner; and a new adventure serial for younger viewers, *Doctor Who*. This last named programme would replace another advertised for 5.15 to 5.45 p.m. called *Emerald Soup*.

Considering the generally gloomy state of mind of most people watching their black and white TV sets that night, the opening shots of *Doctor Who* which showed a policeman examining a police box in a darkened London street were very much in keeping. Indeed, it was not until the emergence of a rather eccentric-looking, white-haired old man from the police box – the now instantly recognisable TARDIS (short for Time And Relative Dimensions In Space: a time machine that appears smaller on the outside than inside) – that it seemed anything untoward might be happening. Just how many older viewers left their sets at this moment feeling drained by the assassination story and seeking some light relief will never be known. But millions more, primarily youngsters, did stay where they were in their living rooms across the nation. At that moment, what would become a Saturday night tradition of watching the dramatic science fiction programme from behind the sofa began . . .

The 'father' of *Doctor Who* – Sydney Newman, Head of Drama at the BBC in 1962.

Verity Lambert, the first producer of *Doctor Who*, with one of her 'stars' at the London Planetarium in 1965.

The extraordinary story of the legend of *Doctor Who* started in the imagination of a man who, like my correspondent in the Rockies, came from Canada. He was the flamboyant, Toronto-born Sydney Newman, who died only last year in his native country, aged eighty. With his swarthy good looks, black hair and pencil moustache, Sydney actually seemed more like a Mexican than a Canadian; but his appearance belied a deep knowledge of broadcasting, and during his career he had a major influence on drama productions in Canada as well as on ITV and BBC following his move to Britain in 1954. He is remembered today as the pioneer of realistic drama – plays about working people in contemporary situations such as *Up The Junction* (1965) and *Cathy Come Home* (1966) – the producer who earned ABC's *Armchair Theatre* a weekly audience of over fifteen million, and the man who dreamed up the basic concept of *Doctor Who*. As one of his employees at the BBC was to say later, 'When Sydney came to us [as Head of Drama in December 1962] he hit us like a whirlwind.'

It was while he was trying to think of a programme to 'fill in' between the end of the BBC's Saturday afternoon sports programme, *Grandstand*, and the evening's light entertainment shows for adults, that he came up with *Doctor Who*. He described his concept in typically robust language: 'I always loved science fiction as a kid and suddenly got the idea of a space machine in which this crotchety old bugger travels backwards and forwards in time. Because he is partly senile, he doesn't know how to work the machine properly and when he tries to get back to his own planet he always ends up somewhere else. And because no one was sure who the old fart was or where he came from, it was obvious to call him *Doctor Who*.'

Newman also thought the Doctor should have a young companion with whom children could identify, plus a couple of adults for older viewers with the possibility of a love interest, too. A series that the whole family could watch, in fact. To put this concept on to the screen, Sydney hired Verity Lambert as the producer, a 24-year-old production assistant who had worked for him at ABC. Educated at Roedean, the vivacious young woman had earlier been a personal assistant to the well-known New York producer and commentator David Susskind. One of today's

leading figures in British television with her own company, Cinema Verity, she had made a strong impression on Sydney because of her determination and ability to argue her point with him. 'She was bright and gutsy and, to use a phrase, full of piss and vinegar.' The expression still makes her smile.

Verity, who now lives in a flat in Holland Park surrounded by her beautiful collection of art deco and art nouveau objects, picks up the story at this point. 'The first thing I saw of *Doctor Who* was literally a page of notes by Sydney. When I actually joined the BBC, a script editor, David Whitaker, was already working on the show. It was to be aimed primarily at children from the ages of nine to fourteen and David had commissioned the first scripts from a writer named Anthony Coburn. Tony, David and I then had several discussions about it all, after which I had to find someone to play the crucial role of this mysterious, complex, crotchety old man. I felt he could be frightening but also kind and, above all, an outsider who did things in his own individual way.

'There were a number of people we were keen on – Cyril Cusack was one possibility, Leslie French another – and we even thought about using a young actor made up to look old to cope with all the demands of the role. Yet all along I was keen on Bill Hartnell because I had seen him do two very different things – the irascible sergeant in *The Army Game* and the talent scout in *This Sporting Life*, trying to cling on to the bright lights. This role was rather touching and it seemed to me that he could be irascible as well as sympathetic at the same time. That is why we chose him.'

Time has, however, played a slight trick with Verity's memory. In fact, the first draft of 'An Unearthly Child' was written by C.E. 'Bunny' Webber, a veteran BBC scriptwriter who had worked for years on the long-running soap, *Compact*. A well-read man, Webber's script proved to be rather too lyrical for the purposes of the series, and was handed over for rewriting to another staff writer, the late Anthony Coburn. Tony, an Australian, efficiently turned the basic plotline, set partly in the Stone Age and partly the present day, into a workable script; he made the Doctor's young companion, Susan, his grand-daughter and also provided the Doctor's time machine with its familiar name, the TARDIS – without, of course, the faintest idea that he, too, was shaping a television legend.

According to Tony's widow Joan, who lives in Herne Bay, Kent, he was always pleased about the success of the show; but he often wondered what *might* have happened if the second story he proposed called 'The Robots' about a group of highly intelligent androids living on a depopulated Earth in the 30th century had been given the go-ahead. As it was, Terry Nation, a writer then better known for his work on comedy shows such as *Hancock's Half Hour*, was approached about doing a story and came up with a script featuring some machines which were the life-support systems of an atrophied race called the Daleks – and the rest, including the success of the series, is history. (See *The Birth of the Daleks*.)

Another apocryphal tale about those early days which needs to be set right is that 'An Unearthly Child' was being recorded in the BBC studios at the time of Kennedy's assassination. In fact that story had already been made into a pilot and, when it met with the disapproval of Sydney Newman, *reshot*; it was actually the second episode of Terry Nation's *The Daleks* entitled 'The Survivors' that was before the cameras on that fateful Friday. Fateful, as it turned out, for both the world and the future of *Doctor Who*.

There was a small group of directors who were also very important in the launching of the series and subsequently became influential figures in TV in their own right including Waris Hussein (who directed 'An Unearthly Child'), Christopher Barry, Douglas Camfield and Julia Smith. Julia, who also sadly died in 1997, directed *The Smugglers*, a four-episode historical story which was the first to go on location outside London in July 1966 when the crew spent a week at Penzance in Cornwall. The tale of piracy was to mark the penultimate story in Hartnell's time as the Doctor and he was, according to Julia, already in failing health and having difficulty with some of his lines. Nonetheless, he was still totally dedicated to the role.

'At times I think he honestly believed he was Doctor Who,' she said later. 'Any actor supporting a series over a number of years gets very weary and his age must have added to this. He was finding it difficult to remember lines [the same applied to Jack Warner] and he was also given very athletic things to do by a lot of the writers. As the Director I had to save him as much as possible.'

The strain of playing the leading role which Julia Smith described was, in fact, to prove a recurring problem for virtually all of William Hartnell's successors – with a variety of consequences as we shall see.

Julia was later to direct the second Doctor, Patrick Troughton, in *The Underwater Menace* (1967) which did not offer her another trip to Cornwall, but instead several days using a huge tank in Ealing Studios for the underwater scenes. After this, her star rose swiftly as the producer of *Z Cars*, *Angels* and *District Nurse*. But it was her creation of *EastEnders* that has etched her name into television history. The series about London life continues to mesmerise millions of viewers; it is often at the centre of arguments about sex, violence and its tackling of disturbing and controversial issues, and generates for the BBC some of its highest ever ratings. In 1993, Julia masterminded a union of *Doctor Who* and *EastEnders* as part of the Children in Need Appeal on 26 November when the TARDIS, complete with the five living Doctors (Jon Pertwee, Tom Baker, Peter Davison, Colin Baker and Sylvester McCoy), landed in Albert Square and encountered the cast of the soap. The episode was also the first to be shown in 3-D with the BBC distributing eight million pairs of special rose- and green-tinted spectacles to be worn by viewers in order to be able to enjoy the full three-dimensional effect.

In the years since this group of people launched *Doctor Who*, it has become more than just a television programme – in the case of my correspondent in Canada, a way of life – and its influence is to be found everywhere in daily living. Only the other day I visited the port of Felixstowe on the Suffolk coast and checked my watch against the Water Clock on the seafront which has as part of its balance mechanism a piece of videotape of 'An Unearthly Child'. And not long ago I found myself driving behind a car with a back window sticker reading 'I Only Brake For Daleks'. That untransmitted pilot of the opening story also emerged to be shown on August Bank Holiday Monday 1991 during a day-long programme to mark the closure of the BBC's studios at Lime Grove where it, along with countless other productions, had been made. As recently as February 1998, *The Times* ran a series of 'Top 100 Cult Moments' and listed at number 14:

> **Doctor Who** Who would have thought that giant pepperpots on castors with pink plungers would capture our imaginations as the most feared aliens in the universe? Yet after their first appearance in *Doctor Who* in 1964, Dalek mania set in. For nearly three decades, children put saucepans on their heads and shouted, 'Ex-ter-min-ate! Ex-ter-min-ate!' And no one minded that these megalomaniacs' plans for world domination could be foiled by a flight of stairs.

(The number one moment in *The Times'* opinion was Marilyn Monroe's scene in *The Seven Year Itch* when a gust of air from a New York subway grating sends her white dress billowing up above her waist.)

Souvenirs from the thirty-five years the series has been in existence are now very collectable – especially battery-operated Daleks, replicas of the TARDIS, models of the famous monsters and even sweets and candy (uneaten, if possible), some of which can command hundreds of pounds. The rarest of all is a full-size Dalek of soft plastic made in 1964 by Scorpion Automatives into which a child could slip and operate the light and probes. Although two of the Daleks were presented to William Hartnell's grandchildren in time for Christmas that year, none ever reached the shops because of a fire which destroyed the company's factory in Northampton and all its stock. The only memento of this rarity is the advertisement illustrated on this page.

Advertisement for the rarest of all *Doctor Who* souvenirs in 1964.

BE A REAL DALEK THIS CHRISTMAS

© BBC EV 1964

A real working full size T.V. Dalek. Be the envy of your friends as you move around and control the lights and probes. The box is also a super Dr. Who Space Ship to the mysterious land of the Daleks. In the shops now.

NOTE TO MOTHER
The Dalek is safe, both inside and outdoor, waterproof & non-inflammable. Vision is good, & being brightly coloured, easily seen by road users. Stores neatly into the box.

MADE BY
Scorpion Automotives

Books, comics and magazines about the Doctor – especially the earlier ones from the sixties and seventies – sell for ever-increasing amounts at fan conventions – and videos of the episodes of *Doctor Who* are one of the BBC's best-selling lines. Most recently, a new CD-Rom game called *Destiny of the Doctors* featuring ten of the Time Lord's most deadly enemies, including Daleks, Cybermen and Yetis, has taken our hero into yet another new dimension thanks to the computer experts at Studio Fish in London who all just happened to be fans! (The appendix to this book, 'Doctor Who Preservation Archive', compiled by one of the leading experts on the show, Jeremy Bentham, provides for the first time a full listing of the availability of all the stories in the various media.)

The popularity of *Doctor Who* is, indeed, generally agreed to be second only to that of *Star Trek* which began later in 1966 and is, of course, still in production for both television and films. No other show, however, has lasted so long as the travels of the Time Lord from Gallifrey, albeit that they are in abeyance at the present moment.

Above all else, however, it is the nine actors who have portrayed the Doctor on television and in movies that have made the concept such a legendary success. Recently an American fan referred to him as 'a rainbow in a black, nasty world'. The men who have provided the colours of this unique rainbow are the subject of this volume marking over thirty-five years of remarkable achievements.

PETER HAINING,
Boxford, Suffolk

The Birth of the Daleks

Terry Nation – 'The Dalek Man' as he became known – was born in South Wales on 8 August 1930 and after briefly working as a salesman in the family furniture business tried his luck as a stand-up comedian. Although his material was good, his delivery was terrible and he shifted his attention to writing for other comedians. After moving to London in 1955 he contributed material to many of the leading performers of the day including Spike Milligan, Frankie Howerd, Ted Ray, Harry Worth, Peter Sellers and Tony Hancock. He was actually working for Hancock when he was approached to write for *Doctor Who* but turned the proposal down because he had very little faith the series would continue past the original thirteen shows and felt 'vaguely insulted' at being asked to write for what he saw as purely a children's show. But when shortly afterwards he had a dispute with Hancock 'and he fired me or I walked out in high dudgeon', Ter (as he was always called by friends) found himself unemployed and revised his original decision. The result was a monster that overshadowed his life but subsequently led to him becoming one of the highest paid freelance television scriptwriters of his generation. He later settled in Los Angeles and in November 1982 wrote to me from his sumptuous house on Avenida de la Herradura in Pacific Palisades describing how the Daleks changed his life. Terry Nation died there after several years of ill-health on 12 March 1997.

'I met with Verity Lambert and outlined a story. I got the go-ahead to get started and at the same time was asked by Eric Sykes if I would go with him to Sweden to do a series of shows on a luxury liner. That was something I wasn't going to miss. So I started writing *Doctor Who* very quickly. Indeed, I wrote one episode per day, completing the serial in a week.

'I did the Swedish stint and then moved on to write episodes for Roger Moore in *The Saint*. Some months later I watched my first episode of *Doctor Who* as it was broadcast. To my surprise it was rather good. In the very final frames of that episode we saw only the "arm" of a Dalek and heard its voice. Then as the credits began to roll my telephone started to ring. Friends asking, "My God, what is it?"

'In the next episode the Daleks really came into their own, and children all over the country were putting cardboard boxes over their heads, sticking their arms out and shouting "Exterminate". Before the

Dalek segment ended, I was receiving literally vans full of mail. Thousands of letters. The Daleks were on their way to becoming a folk hero to English children.

'To me the Daleks were "Them". They represent for so many people so many different things, but they all see them as government, as official-dom, as that unhearing, unthinking, blanked-out face of authority that will destroy you because it *wants* to destroy you.

'There were many rewards and pleasures to come from the Daleks, but the one I treasure most was when I learned the word DALEK had been included in a new edition of the *Oxford English Dictionary*. Not only had I created a monster, I had created a word. What writer could ask for more.'

Terry Nation has also disclaimed a story that he got the word for his monsters from the spine of a volume of an encyclopaedia on his bookshelf marked DAL – LEK. 'It was a piece of pure invention to satisfy the press,' he explained, 'as anyone could have found out by checking that there has never been an encyclopaedia covering those particular letters!' His description of the monsters in the script was also graphically simple: 'Hideous machine-like creatures, they are legless, moving on a round base. They have no human features. A lens on a flexible shaft acts as an eye. Arms with mechanical grips for hands.' It was to be the inventive skill of a BBC designer, Raymond Cusick, who turned this vision into an even more terrifying reality . . .

Terry Nation, the scriptwriter who dreamed up the Daleks.

The Doctor
Flies In

? The sun was high in a clear blue sky on the afternoon of Saturday 4 September 1965 when the TARDIS dropped in to the International Air Show at Farnborough in Hampshire. Many thousands of onlookers including a sea of children's faces were looking up as the police box familiar to every viewer of *Doctor Who* floated down to land on one of the Royal Aircraft Establishment's runways. As the TARDIS touched down, an aircraft flying overhead banked away – but not a single eye followed its departure.

What happened next was almost like magic, especially to the younger onlookers. From behind the TARDIS emerged a jeep and there sitting beside the driver was a familiar figure with long, white hair curling from under an astrakhan hat, wrapped in a cape and waving a stick. As the vehicle pulled away from the police box, it seemed to all intents and purposes as if the Doctor had stepped out of his time machine to join the waiting crowds at the air show.

Farnborough, which has been the laboratory of British aviation since 1906, has seen many extraordinary events, but few more unusual or eagerly awaited than the appearance of the first Doctor in September 1965. It was a year in which space travel had grabbed many of the headlines – the Americans and Russians had both sent planetary probes to Mars, and on 3 June, Major Edward White had become the first American to walk in space. Just two days before the opening of the show, the national press had also carried photographs of the first rivet-hole being driven into the fuselage assembly of Concorde – the Anglo-French supersonic aircraft then being built at the British Aircraft Corporation's factory at Filton,

WILLIAM HARTNELL

ACTOR: **William Hartnell (1908–75)**

TIME-SPAN: **1963–6**

CHARACTERISTICS: **An enigmatic, haughty, frequently bad-tempered old man. Eccentric, irascible and occasionally intolerant, he had a passion for travelling into Earth's past history.**

APPEARANCE: **His black frock coat gave him a late-Victorian/Edwardian look. Underneath this he wore a fawn waistcoat, a wing-collared shirt and neat, black necktie. His check trousers were tapered and always carefully creased. The first Doctor wore a long white wig and on the small finger of his left hand a ring with a large blue stone. He was also sometimes seen wearing an opera cape and scarf, an astrakhan fur hat and a monocle.**

Bristol. This now famous airliner which, it was claimed, would fly at 1,450 mph and make a 'gigantic leap forward in aviation history', would also subsequently appear in *Doctor Who* during the era of the fifth Doctor.

As for television, 1965 was the year of *The Telegoons*, *Perry Mason* and *Dr Finlay's Casebook*; cigarette advertising was banned from the screen 'because it is an effective form of advertising for adolescents'; and Mary Whitehouse announced her 'Clean Up TV' campaign by founding the National Viewers' and Listeners' Association to tackle what she considered to be 'BBC bad taste and irresponsibility'. The self-appointed censor would later become a regular critic of what she saw as scenes of violence in *Doctor Who*.

The original Doctor looking characteristically stern.

William Hartnell was by that September something of a veteran of personal appearances. But this event was particularly special for him because the RAF had gone to the trouble of building a full-size TARDIS from lightweight plastic sheets over a frame of aluminium poles which had been dropped from an aircraft by a parachute to herald his arrival. When it landed close to a runway, the illusion that the Doctor had been travelling in it was completed by his surprise appearance in the jeep.

All those present that day – of whom I was one – remember that it did seem as if the star of the time-travel TV series had dropped in from some far-distant planet. I was then a trade press journalist and had been invited to the air show by *Flight* magazine. Although I had watched *Doctor Who* as often as my work allowed, I had been asked by the assistant editor of my magazine to try and get Hartnell's autograph for his young son who had never missed an episode. I remember I had to stand in a queue for quite a long time to meet the Doctor, but he sat for at least two hours until everyone waiting had been satisfied, each getting a smile of his hazel-brown eyes and a signature. After that, he was whisked away by his hosts and the last I saw of him was as he disappeared into an RAF hospitality tent where I am sure he had a well-earned gin and tonic or two.

It was not until years later that I thought again about this man who had made his acting reputation as a figure of menace, but become famous as the first Doctor, when I started writing about the series. It was

then almost a decade after his death and twenty years since *Doctor Who* had first been shown.

On that day at Farnborough, to which Hartnell had been driven with his wife Heather from their seventeenth-century home in Mayfield, Sussex, he spoke to journalists about playing the Doctor. By one of the many curious coincidences that seem to have attached themselves to the show, it was to be almost exactly a year to the day that the news of his departure from the series was announced. But such thoughts were far from Bill's mind as he enunciated a number of well-rehearsed comments which were duly reported in the Monday editions of the national press.

'I'm the High Lama of the planet,' he told the *Daily Mirror*. 'Although I portray a mixed-up old man, I have discovered I can hypnotise children. Hypnotism goes with the fear of the unknown. I communicate fear to children because they don't know where I'm going to take them. This frightens them and is the attraction of the series. I am hypnotised by *Doctor Who* myself. When I look at the script I find it unbelievable. So I allow myself to be hypnotised by it, otherwise I would have nothing to do with it.'

How closely he identified with the role was revealed in another comment. 'Everyone calls me Doctor Who and I feel like him,' he said. 'I get

William Hartnell surrounded by fans of all ages at the Farnborough Air Show, accompanied by his wife, Heather, in sunglasses.

letters addressed to me as "Mr Who" and even "Uncle Who". I love being this eccentric old man. I love it when my granddaughter, Judith, calls me "barmy old grandad". I can see the series going on for five years at least . . .'

Over thirty years after that memorable weekend, we know that William Hartnell seriously underestimated the period of time *Doctor Who* would last, just as we know a great deal more about the man himself. His charming wife, Heather, was my own primary source of information when I first began to write about the series, and no one could have been more helpful and honest about Bill's part in the success story. Subsequently, members of the cast and crew of *Doctor Who* have filled in details of those early days. Other facts have also been brought to light by the tireless research of Bill's granddaughter, Judith. She is now an actress, director and writer and calls herself Jessica Carney to avoid confusion with another Equity member. (Her husband, Terry Carney, was for many years Hartnell's manager.)

Throughout his career, William Henry Hartnell maintained that he had been born on 8 January 1908 at the village of Seaton in Devon where his forebears had been farmers for over 300 years. Although it is true that his mother came from Devon, and he spent several school holidays with an aunt who still lived there, his birth certificate at Somerset House proves otherwise. The man who became the first Doctor was born in London in Regent Square near St Pancras Station, the illegitimate child of Lucy Hartnell and a father whose particulars are left blank on the certificate. Granddaughter Jessica who first looked up the birth certificate believes that the stigma of being illegitimate was one of the formative influences on William Hartnell's life. Despite efforts that Bill himself made later in his life, the identity of his father has never been discovered.

Heather Hartnell met Bill when she was an aspiring actress named Heather McIntyre and both were touring in Noel Coward plays. She says that he never spoke of his childhood, though she had the impression it had been unhappy. He had apparently been an unruly child and occasionally in trouble with the law. Bill was then taken under the wing of an art connoisseur named Hugh Blaker who encouraged his interest in the arts and also helped him to get his first job as a stable lad at Epsom. Although he trained as a jockey, Bill grew too tall (5 ft 8 ins) and sensed the turf would never provide him with a livelihood. It did, though, arouse his interest in gambling on horse racing which he followed enthusiastically (and not always wisely!) throughout the rest of his life.

Instead, Hartnell decided to try and emulate his great hero Charlie Chaplin and become an actor. Once again, Hugh Blaker helped him to get into the famous Italia Conti Drama School, where his fellow students included Roger Livesey and Jack Hawkins. Within a year he had demonstrated a real talent for acting and in 1925 was signed up by Sir Frank Benson's company.

'I went to work for Sir Frank about the same time as the late Robert Donat,' he said in an interview in 1975. 'I was paid twenty-five shillings a week and played nothing but Shakespeare. Later I discovered I could make people laugh, and toured in a whole series of glorious dead-pan comedies – which I think are the funniest of all.'

In the thirties, 'Billy' Hartnell as he was known got his first experience of film-making in a number of 'quota quickies' including the comic fantasy, *I'm An Explosive* (1933) about a liquid which turns a man into a human explosive, *Swinging The Lead* (1935) where a criminal gang get hold of a personality-changing drug, and *Midnight at Madame Tussaud's* (1937) in which Hartnell appeared as a Chaplinesque reporter covering the events when a financier bets he can spend a night in the Chamber of Horrors.

Unfortunately, the Second World War put a stop to Bill's film career just when he was on the verge of securing a contract to work in Hollywood. Instead he found himself in the Army Tank Corps where, according to another 1965 interview, he served eleven months as a private before suffering a nervous breakdown and being discharged.

'The strain of training was too much. I spent twelve weeks in an Army hospital and came out with a terrible stutter,' he recalled. 'The colonel said, "Better get back to the theatre – you're no bloody good here." So I had to start all over again. I was still only a spit and a cough in the profession and now I had a stutter which scared the life out of me. It was a hard battle to overcome, but if the Army did anything for me it gave an insight into the NCO parts I played later.'

By now married to Heather, Bill managed to secure work in a number of wartime films including *They Flew Alone* (1942), *The Goose Steps Out* (1943) with Will Hay playing a comic spy, and *The Bells Go Down* (1944) about the community spirit in London during the Blitz. Then in 1947 he landed a role in Roy Boulting's version of *Brighton Rock* by Graham Greene, a brutal and realistic story of gang warfare in Brighton. By a twist of fate, that same year Bill played a police inspector in the Rex Harrison thriller *Escape* in which Patrick Troughton also appeared as a shepherd.

Heather remembers *Brighton Rock* as a turning point in both their lives. 'He played opposite Richard Attenborough who was then aged seventeen and it was a smash hit,' she said. 'Dallow was a racecourse heavy and the first tough guy he had played. From then on Bill became renowned as the tough guy, getting parts as sergeants, detectives, crooks, prison officers and so on.

'Curiously, though, the first thing he did for television was quite different. It happened before Independent Television went on the air and they were stock-piling material for the future. He played a man who trained a blind person to use a guide dog. Bill was sent to a training centre in Bristol where he was shown how such people were trained. While he was there he got to know the trainers and how they worked with the dogs. He admired them greatly and thereafter Guide Dogs for the Blind became his favourite charity.'

William Hartnell also went on working in the theatre and enjoyed a four-year run in the hugely successful version of Hugh Hastings' *Seagulls Over Sorrento* in which he appeared as Petty Officer Herbert. One fellow actor who saw the play at the Apollo was so impressed by Bill's performance that he wrote him a letter of admiration. The man was Peter Cushing, who would later be the first person to play the Doctor in the cinema.

By the sixties, Bill – now in his late fifties – had become anxious to play character roles to extend his range. It was a fateful decision and one that would lead to his most famous role of all, as Heather Hartnell remembered vividly.

'The film was called *This Sporting Life* [1963] and starred Richard Harris. Bill was cast as Johnson: this rather ragged, pathetic old man who acts as a rugby talent scout and puts Richard Harris on the road to success. It was the first time he had been cast in such a part and he made a tremendous success of it. It was as a result of this that he was offered the role in *Doctor Who*.

'I will always remember when our son-in-law, Terry, who was then Bill's agent, rang up one day in July 1963. He said he had this script he wanted Bill to read. Terry was a bit apprehensive because it was for a children's serial in which he would have to play an old professor with long white hair who is a bit round the bend. I said I thought Bill would love it if it was not another tough guy part. Well, when Bill sat down to read the script he never spoke a word until he was finished. Then he said,

"My goodness, I want this part!" He saw straight away that there was something very different about *Doctor Who* and he wanted to be part of it. If there was anything about it he was sorry about, it was that the man was rather grumpy and he would have liked to put more comedy into the part right from the start.'

Bill himself recalled that day in an interview marking the tenth anniversary of *Doctor Who*. 'It was like manna from heaven getting away from all the barrack-room spit and polish. The original Doctor was pig-headed and irascible, certainly, but there was also an element of magic in him – and that was what I tried to bring out. I remember one actor said to me, "This show won't last more than six weeks" but I knew – I *knew* – it was going to be a tremendous success. I was laughed at and mocked a good deal for my faith, but I believed in it. I think I represented to children a cross between the Wizard of Oz and Father Christmas.'

Verity Lambert and Waris Hussein, the young Indian director who made the first *Doctor Who* story, immediately impressed Hartnell with their dedication to the new series, displaying a professionalism he thought was

William Hartnell with his three co-stars, Carol Ann Ford, Jacqueline Hall and William Russell, in *The Sensorites.*

mature beyond their ages, both still in their mid-twenties. Perhaps even more than them, he realised that his tendency to be cantankerous, his occasional lack of tolerance and unpredictability, mixed with a generosity of spirit, sense of humour and ability to get his own way were just what the part required. Bill helped in selecting the items of clothing for the Doctor and it remains a mistaken impression among some fans that the long white hair was Hartnell's own – it was a *wig*.

When it came to making the series, Bill brought to bear all the professionalism that he had developed over the years on the stage, in films and, most recently in the hit comedy television series, *The Army Game*, in which he had played the aptly-named Sergeant-Major Bullimore. This especially was an image he wanted to dispel. He was also keen that whatever science he was called upon to perform in the Doctor's name should look realistic even if it *was* fantastic, although he did not like too much scientific dialogue and would sometimes insist on bits of technical jargon being removed from the script.

Bill also devised a method of operating the TARDIS controls which he would never deviate from because he knew his young viewers were watching carefully and would pick up on any discrepancies. This tendency to be pernickety either amused or irritated the various directors he worked with on the series, as Julia Smith recalled:

'Rehearsals were sometimes held up for ages because he had to tell me exactly what happened to the TARDIS if he pressed a particular button. I couldn't do anything about it . . . he was away in never-never land.'

Bill also quickly developed an affinity with his three co-stars: Carol Ann Ford, as his fifteen-year-old granddaughter, Susan; and William Russell and Jacqueline Hall who played Ian Chesterton and Barbara Wright, her two teachers from Coal Hill school, London, who became unwitting companions in the first Doctor's meandering odyssey. Indeed, he grew to regard them as 'family' and was not above issuing instructions rather like a stern Victorian father when he thought things were going wrong. He was also in the habit of reprimanding *any* actors who showed signs of becoming frivolous.

The advent of the Daleks in the second story in the series was, of course, what sealed *Doctor Who*'s success – though Bill was never a great admirer of them.

'I think they are too mechanical,' he said in a rather caustic statement in 1966, 'and they've been overplayed. I don't mean to undermine their

(Above) The Doctor
confronted by two
enemies in the *Planet
of the Zarbi* and
(left) meeting the
peace-loving
Menoptera in the *TV
Comic* version of the
story which appeared
in March 1965.

success, but I don't think they could survive on their own. They need Doctor Who to outwit and confound their every move, he is a continual challenge and frustration to them. I much prefer real people – I would like to see some characters from children's books in the series.'

Some of this bitterness may have been occasioned by the accident he suffered while rehearsing *The Dalek Invasion of Earth* in October 1964. While he was being carried down a ramp on a stretcher from a Dalek spaceship, the supports gave way and he fell badly on his spine, suffering temporary paralysis. Although he suffered no permanent damage, Bill was prevented from working for several days.

He did, though, very much enjoy making *The Web Planet* by Bill Strutton in February 1965 which was about a barren planet named Vortis that rather resembled the moon, where the hostile, ant-like Zarbi were at war with the benevolent, butterfly-like Menoptera.

'I was not overkeen on the Zarbi, but the beautiful Menoptera were different,' he said. 'I thought they showed the potential *Doctor Who* has to present that all is not evil in the universe – although I have very little interest in finding out for real. If man was meant to meet the Daleks, or whatever lives on other planets, he would have been born there.'

The Wet Planet was an extraordinarily bold production for such a new series, because apart from the Doctor and his three companions there was not a single humanoid creature in the story. All the other actors and actresses were completely swathed in special costumes. The Zarbi outfits were made in three sections of heavy vinyl with wires inside for the actors to manipulate the pincers and took at least twenty minutes to get into. The Menoptera in their black catsuits ringed with yellow fur and large, plastic wings were also called upon to 'fly' in a climactic battle scene with the Zarbi. This sequence was staged at Ealing Film Studios using a theatrical invention called Kirby's Flying Ballet. In order to create the effect, a harness arrangement was worn by the actors under their costumes and linked to a steel wire and a system of pulleys. A stage hand would then pull the other end of the wire lifting each actor into the air and creating the impression they were flying.

The story was a triumph for designer Barry Newberry and the BBC Costume and Visual Effects Department, and the first episode achieved a record audience in excess of over three million viewers. Despite its success, though, the effects were just too expensive to consider a return of the insects, and it remains to this day unique in the series.

Interestingly, *The Web Planet* inspired some of the earliest souvenirs associated with *Doctor Who* apart from the Daleks. Indeed, it was hoped in some quarters of the BBC that the Zarbi and Menoptera might prove as popular with children as the 'evil pepperpots'. Licences were granted for Zarbi and Menoptera badges to be manufactured by Plastoid Ltd from polystyrene with the creatures etched in gold paint, and they were also featured in the early comic strip adventures of the Doctor in *TV Comic* and in the first and now very rare *Dr Who Annual* written by script editor David Whitaker for World Distributors Ltd in 1965. But the same clamour for souvenirs that had greeted the Daleks did not materialise this time. In fact, during the rest of Hartnell's time as the Doctor, only plastic models of the Mechanoids from *The Chase* – also created by Terry Nation – were manufactured by Herts Plastic Moulders Ltd on the same scale as the Daleks.

Within a year of the launch of *Doctor Who*, William Hartnell was a household name, receiving fan letters from all over Britain and places as far away as Australia, Africa and the West Indies where the series was now being shown. All of these he answered with the help of Heather, often enclosing a signed photograph.

'Some people really began to take the series literally,' he reflected later. 'I got letters from boys swotting for O-levels asking complicated questions about the time-ratio and the TARDIS. Doctor Who might have been able to answer them, but I'm afraid I couldn't.'

Hartnell had, in fact, become the first recipient of the kind of requests for information about the series and its actors which would later develop into a mania with certain fans.

By April 1966, the strain of working on *Doctor Who* was beginning to tell on William Hartnell. For years he had been a heavy smoker and spirit drinker – though he absolutely refused to allow the Doctor to be seen doing either during the series – and the year-round schedule was taking its toll, as he confided to Jack Bell of the *Daily Mirror* on 23 April during a break from filming *The Gunfighters*.

'I want a change in conditions from the BBC,' he said. 'It's not a question of money – they pay me very well, though I work bloody hard for it. But you can never escape from the character – that's the agony of being Doctor Who. I did the first fifty-three weeks without a break; now I get nine weeks off a year but it takes me two weeks to unwind from the part. I would like something like *Dr Finlay's Casebook* – it runs for

twenty-six episodes and then gets a twenty-six week break. I know my irritation spills over into arguments with directors. Once or twice I've put my foot down with a new director and told him, "I know how to play Doctor Who and I don't want you to intrude on it or alter it".'

Bill went on even more bluntly: '*Doctor Who* has given me a certain neurosis – and it is not easy for my wife to cope with. I get a little agitated, and it makes me a little irritable with people. In fact, Doctor Who seems to be taking over.'

In actual fact, it was something far more basic than the role which was taking over Bill: he was suffering from the onset of arteriosclerosis. The early signs had been there when he started finding it difficult to remember lines and then getting angry at anything that disturbed him. He became

A photograph, taken
at rehearsal by Ray
Cusick, of Hartnell and
the mechanical
enemies who helped
to make him famous.

prone to temper outbursts and a certain resentment towards anybody new on the programme. When William Russell and Jacqueline Hill announced they were leaving the series – to be followed by a similar statement from Verity Lambert – Hartnell felt this deeply. His subsequent companions were the castaway Vicki from the planet Dido (Maureen O'Brien, 1965), the astronaut Steven Taylor (Peter Purves, 1965–6), the Greek hand-maiden, Katarina (Adrienne Hill, 1965), the cheeky Cockney teenager Dodo Chaplet (Jackie Lane, 1965), 'dolly bird' Polly (Anneke Wills 1966–7) and seaman, Ben Jackson (Michael Craze, 1966–7). When they, one after another, left with the exception of Anneke and Michael, he found coming to rehearsals no longer the pleasure it had once been, compounded by his failing health.

Heather Hartnell remembered this time well. 'Finally, when Bill had to leave *Doctor Who* because of his ill-health it broke his heart. Having said to the press that it was going to run for five years he was determined to be true to his word. But he kept forgetting his lines and his legs were beginning to give way. By the end of 1966 he was getting steadily weaker, mentally and physically. That is the awful thing about arteriosclerosis: as the arteries close up, the flow of blood is weakened to the brain as well as the limbs.

'We were both delighted when Patrick Troughton took over the show, but after a time Bill stopped watching because it upset him emotionally. He regretted that it was no longer a programme for children and hardly saw any of Jon Pertwee's stories. He was pleased to think the show had gone on so long and when he did *The Three Doctors* in 1972 it seemed to take ten years off his illness. He had this lovely final line, too, as he looked at Pat and Jon: "So this is what I've come to – a dandy and a clown!"'

It was Heather who also pointed out to me that Bill had actually envisaged the day when he might leave the series some years earlier and suggested to the BBC that the Doctor might have a 'son' to carry on his exploits. A letter he wrote outlining this idea and his own version of the events when he left the series is reprinted in this book. (See *The Son of Who?*)

However, when William Hartnell left *Doctor Who* he did not stop acting altogether. He appeared in several plays; a pantomime, *Puss in Boots*, in which he played Buskin the Cobbler but was billed as 'Television's Original Doctor Who', and made what proved to be his last movie appearance in November 1970 in a cameo role in *The Abominable Doctor Phibes* starring Vincent Price.

Bill died peacefully aged 67 in hospital in Maidstone, Kent on 23 April 1975. The following day's newspapers all carried obituaries which focused on his role as the Doctor, and several gave him credit for demonstrating such versatility after years as the 'hard man' of the screen. His wife Heather forgave him the years of irritability and heavy drinking, and helped promote his memory whenever approached by fans of the series or writers like myself. Right until the day of her death in December 1984, she retained the fondest memories of the series and her most precious possession was a little solid gold TARDIS on a chain which Bill had had made specially for her by a London jeweller. On the top of this glowed a tiny green emerald representing the machine's light which, like the appeal of the programme that William Hartnell launched, has never dimmed.

The Son of Who?

William Hartnell wrote the following letter from his cottage in Mayfield on 13 August 1968, in reply to a suggestion that perhaps there might have been a second Doctor working alongside him to ensure the continuation of the series. The letter is also interesting for its version of why he left the series.

Your letter to me I found most interesting. But, first let me say, you could not have two Dr Whos. I myself suggested this some four years ago, by having a son and calling it *The Son of Dr Who*.

The idea was for me to have a wicked son, both looked alike and both had a Tardis and travelled in outer space. In fact, I would have had to play a dual role when meeting up with him.

This idea was not acceptable to the BBC. So I forgot it very quickly. But I still think it would have worked and been exciting to the children. It is not many people that get the ideas or write about them.

However, it is a long time ago now, and I think my hurt has healed, although I must say it is engraved on my heart. I left [*Doctor Who*] because we did not see eye to eye over the stories and too much evil entered into the spirit of the thing. It was noted and spelled out to me as a children's programme and I wanted it to stay as such but, I'm afraid the BBC had other ideas. So did I, so I left.

That is all there is to it. I'm sorry to write this, but there is nothing I can do about it now. I didn't willingly give up the part, but BBC planners forced me to retire. Say no more.

Yours sincerely,
William Hartnell

The Eccentric Inventor

? The distance between the Isle of Dogs in the River Thames to the town of Whitstable on the Kent coast where London's great river heads into the North Sea is less than 50 miles as the crow flies. The two quite dissimilar locations, one in the heart of Docklands and the other an attractive seaside resort famous for its oysters, are, though, inextricably linked by Peter Cushing, the second actor to play Doctor Who in two movies made in the mid-sixties. For he had one of his most memorable filmic moments while shooting *The Daleks: Invasion Earth 2150 AD*, on the Isle of Dogs, and he lived for many years in Whitstable where I met him to talk about his career in acting and his place in the Doctor Who legend.

With a smile flickering across his narrow, lined face he recalled a scene shot on the water's edge of the Isle of Dogs where he and his co-star, Bernard Cribbins, had been captured by a Dalek and two of their dehumanised Robomen. 'It was a pretty cold morning and the Thames was freezing so none of us was anxious to get our feet wet,' Peter said. 'But the poor chap working the Dalek had to stand inside to operate the thing while it was in the water. The Dalek was on the end of a pulley system of wires and these were supposed to pull it out of the water when Bernard and I were captured. Well, once the Dalek was in the water, it kept getting stuck every time the prop men tried to pull it out so we had to do the scene over and over again until they got it right. The poor man inside was pretty cold and damp by the time we finished the scene. It was only afterwards that I wondered to myself how a Dalek, which isn't the most mobile thing on dry land as it is, could have come to be in the Thames in the first place!'

PETER CUSHING

ACTOR: Peter Cushing (1913–94)

TIME-SPAN: 1965–6

CHARACTERISTICS: An ingenious inventor with a strong moral sense. He was intelligent and sprightly during his first battle with the Daleks, but had aged somewhat by the time of his second encounter, though he remained courageous throughout both adventures.

APPEARANCE: He wore a long corduroy jacket over a floral waistcoat and a neat cravat stuck with a pin around the neck of his white shirt. The Doctor had striped trousers and leather boots and sported a gold watch and chain across his waistcoat. He, too, wore a white wig, but also had a neatly clipped moustache.

The vista from the row of terraced houses on Seaview across West Beach, Whitstable where Peter lived is very different from the grimy reaches of the London river – quite stunning, in fact. Away to the right are the tossing waves of the North Sea, while to the left lies the mouth of the Thames, with the coastline of the Isle of Sheppey partly obscuring the bright lights of Southend-on-Sea in the distance on the Essex coast. Number 3, Westview, is a three-storey building situated at the very edge of the shingle beach along which Peter loved to stroll when he was not away filming – sometimes with the scarf he had worn in the second film and kept as a souvenir tightly wrapped around his neck. Today, the town has a permanent reminder of their much-loved resident who died in 1994 in the shape of a handsome wooden bench-seat at Keam's Yard, the very spot where he so often paused to enjoy the view. Referred to as either 'Peter's Seat' or 'Cushing's View' it bears the inscription, 'Presented by Helen and Peter Cushing who love Whitstable and its people so very much, 1992.'

Peter Cushing and Bernard Cribbins filming a scene on the banks of the Thames, on the Isle of Dogs, for *The Daleks: Invasion Earth 2150 AD* (1966).

Peter was, in fact, the most courteous and sincere man I have ever known and was certainly not uttering the usual actor's platitudes when he said that his two appearances as the Doctor were among his favourite roles, despite the fact that he was taken seriously ill while making the second picture and was far from well when he completed it. But his lifelong determination always to give the best possible performances drove him on – just as it did William Hartnell – in order not to disappoint his fans.

I co-authored a book with Peter, *Tales of a Monster Hunter*, in 1977 and during the course of writing this we met several times at Browns Hotel in London where he liked to stay when filming at Shepperton or Elstree, and once at Whitstable. Among our topics of conversation were the two films, *Dr Who and the Daleks* (1965) and *The Daleks: Invasion Earth 2150 AD* (1966), as well as his thoughts about playing the character who was not then the popular icon he is today.

'Playing Doctor Who was one of the most heroic parts one could wish for,' he said. 'He was already tremendously popular on television with children, and I thought it might be possible to make him just as popular with older audiences. I certainly did not want to copy the way Bill Hartnell played the role. I sensed the Doctor was a man of many parts.'

Peter was quite surprised to have been offered the role in the first place, having assumed that William Hartnell would play it when the project was announced. But, in fact, the same thing had once happened to him.

Ten years earlier he had starred as Winston Smith in the famous BBC adaptation of George Orwell's novel *1984*. (In fact, the story was initially broadcast live on the evening of Sunday 12 December 1954 and so shocked a number of viewers that they tried to stop the repeat on Thursday night. A group of five MPs also tabled a motion in the House of Commons 'deploring the tendency evident in recent BBC television programmes, notably on Sunday evenings, to pander to sexual and sadistic tastes'. The repeat went ahead with a warning to viewers beforehand – remarks which mirrored those later directed at the *Doctor Who* series.

The irony of the situation was not lost on Peter. 'It seems a shame that Bill isn't doing the film because he's so good in the part,' he told the press in 1965 with typical generosity. 'I remember how I felt when they were casting for the film version of *1984* [in 1955]. I was so keen to repeat my TV role, but they gave it to Edmund O'Brien instead. The next thing is I'm playing Doctor Who while Bill is on TV. All part of life's ups and downs!'

Grappling with a
Dalek: Peter Cushing
and Roy Castle in the
first of the two
movies, *Dr Who and
the Daleks* (1965).

Peter Wilton Cushing certainly had ups and downs in his life which began on 26 May 1913 at Kenley, near Purley in Surrey. He was the second son of a reticent quantity surveyor and a rather domineering mother who, because she already had a son and had always wanted a girl, insisted on letting his hair grow long and curly and dressing him in frocks for the first years of his life. Later, he was kept in short trousers until his late teens and had a reputation, he said, of being a 'cry-baby'.

Because Peter was somewhat embarrassed about all this he liked to lose himself in the fantasy worlds of comics like *Puck*, containing the adventures of 'Rob the Rover and his Wondrous Amphibious Aeroplane', and the *Gem* and *Magnet* full of Charles Hamilton's stories of Billy Bunter, Harry Wharton & Co and Rookwood School. While he was young, he also began a lifelong fascination with collecting model soldiers.

It was an aunt who had once been on the stage who stirred the first thoughts in Peter Cushing's mind about becoming an actor – after all, he told himself, he had spent the first few years of his life 'in costume'. His first appearance was as a 'devilish little goblin' in a production at his Dulwich Primary School. Later, some trips to the local cinema where the cowboy star Tom Mix became his hero, plus all the fun to be had playing games of 'let's pretend' with his brother David, strengthened this ambition.

While at Purley County Secondary School, one of Peter's masters, D.J. Davies, was the first to detect a latent acting talent in him and encouraged him to take part in school productions, including an ambitious version of *The Rivals* in which he appeared as Sir Anthony Absolute. When he left school, however, Cushing senior had other ideas for his future and found him a job in the Drawing Office of the Surveyor's Department at Coulsdon and Purley Urban District Council.

Undeterred, Peter joined a local amateur dramatic society and then managed to get a place at the Guildhall School of Music and Drama in London whereupon he gave up his job with the council, much to the dismay of his parents. His first professional job was in June 1936 as assistant stage manager at Bill Fraser's Connaught Theatre in Worthing and he made his acting debut that same year in J.B. Priestley's *Cornelius*.

Then in January 1939, with just three years' experience in weekly repertory behind him, Peter decided to try his luck by going to Hollywood. By an astonishing stroke of good fortune he landed a role in *The Man in the Iron Mask* directed by James Whale (of *Frankenstein* fame) and followed this by getting another part in the Laurel and Hardy comedy,

A Chump at Oxford (1940). That same year he was cast in his first major role in *Vigil in the Night*, co-starring with Carole Lombard.

By now war was raging in Europe, and Peter decided to return to Britain. He was, however, exempted from military service because of torn knee ligaments and a perforated ear-drum, and so joined ENSA ('Every Night Something Awful'), the theatrical company which travelled around entertaining the troops. It was a fateful decision, for in May 1942 while touring in Noel Coward's *Private Lives* he met and fell in love with an actress named Helen Beck. They were married in April 1943 at Kensington Registry Office and their love was one of the sustaining forces of Peter's life – both while Helen was alive and after her death in January 1971. The play which brought them together was, in fact, the first of two coincidences that link Peter to William Hartnell – who had also, of course, met *his* wife while touring in a production of the Coward play.

'I actually saw Bill Hartnell in a stage production of *Seagulls Over Sorrento* in the early fifties and was so impressed that I wrote him a fan letter,' said Peter. 'I can't quite remember what I said, but I do remember that he was very good as Petty Officer Herbert. It was curious that I should later take over his role in the *Doctor Who* films.'

In fact, thanks to Jessica Carney, who kept a copy of Peter Cushing's letter to her grandfather, we *do* know the contents:

'May I just send my most sincere congratulations on your excellent performance on Wednesday evening,' Cushing wrote. 'It was an evening of joyous excitement – and your contribution to the general success was very great indeed. It was possible to see the P.O.'s mind working! Everything was so true and authentic. Thank you for another faultless performance and for a most unforgettable night in the theatre.' (As a matter of interest, Peter himself appeared in 1956 in a BBC radio production of *Seagulls Over Sorrento* as Able Seaman Badger.)

Although William Hartnell must have been pleased by this letter (as the evidence that he kept it suggests), how he reacted to Cushing taking his role on the screen is unknown. Whether the BBC would not or could not allow Hartnell to appear because of his contract – or whether Cushing got the casting because he was the bigger star – will now never be resolved. One suspects the latter to be true.

It was the growth of drama on television in the mid-fifties which made Peter Cushing into a household name and earned him the title 'The Horror Man of the BBC' which, in a varied form, he never lost. His first major part on TV was as the aloof and elegant Mr Darcy in Jane Austen's *Pride and Prejudice* which helped him to win Outstanding Actor of the Year in the National Television Awards, 1953–4. It was a far step from those childhood days of 'dressing up', and gave him a great sense of personal satisfaction.

However, the furore which greeted Peter's performance in *1984* astounded him. It also marked him down as an actor to watch and when Hammer Films began their extraordinary series of Gothic horror films with *The Curse of Frankenstein* in 1956, they offered him what was to prove the first of six appearances as Baron Frankenstein. The following year he became forever associated with another role, that of the vampire hunter, Professor Van Helsing in *Dracula*, playing opposite his great friend, Christopher Lee, the vampire count.

None of Peter's work to that date had, however, quite prepared him for the role of the Doctor when he was offered the starring role in *Dr Who and the Daleks* in 1965. He had certainly played medical men and scientists before – such as the lead in *The Curious Dr Robson* (Q Theatre, 1946) and the myopic, disillusioned scientist in *Number Three* (BBC, 1953) – but now he was being asked to play a man who combined both qualities *and* had his own time machine. The Doctor of the movies was to be more of an eccentric, Earthbound inventor than the one on TV, and a much more jovial figure. He was said to have constructed his time machine from pieces of equipment bought at everyday electrical shops.

'The first thing I had to do was get the degree of eccentricity of the character right,' he said. 'I did watch some of the Bill Hartnell serials and saw that he played the character as a rather grumpy old man who seemed to be intolerant of human weaknesses. I wanted to make Doctor Who a more likeable and sprightly figure. A clever inventor who believes he can outwit the Daleks with science.'

Among the television stories that Peter had a chance to watch were two, *The Savages* and (appropriately) *The War Machines*, both written by a man with whom he had already worked, Ian Stuart Black. Black, who died in 1997 after a prolific career as novelist, playwright and screenwriter, was the creator of *Danger Man* starring Patrick McGoohan in 1959 which became the first really successful British TV export to the USA (where it was retitled *Secret Agent*). He also wrote a best-selling novel, *High Bright Sun* which was filmed in 1962 with Dirk Bogarde. Peter had worked with him in 1954 when he co-starred with Sheila Sim in Black's comedy, *The Soldier and the Lady* which ran for several months in the West End.

Of all Ian Stuart Black's contributions to *Doctor Who* (he also wrote a third story, *The Macra Terror* for Patrick Troughton in 1967), Peter said *The War Machines* gave him the best pointers for his portrayal. Originally to be called *Doctor Who and the Computers*, its theme of omnipotent machines threatening to take over the Earth made it the first story in the series with a wholly contemporary setting. Sadly, both *The Savages* and *The Macra Terror* were wiped by the BBC in 1974.

The idea of bringing the Doctor and the Daleks to the cinema in the full glory of Technicolor was that of film maker Milton Subotsky, who heretofore had made a speciality of 'anthology' films like *Doctor Terror's House of Horrors* (1964) based on short horror stories. (He did, in fact, later employ me for a time as a consultant.) Sensing the public interest in the characters, Subotsky approached the BBC in the autumn of 1964 and arranged a three-picture deal which would begin with a revised version of the original Dalek story, *The Dead Planet* by Terry Nation. Assisted by Nation and script editor David Whitaker, he decided to reveal in the new storyline that the Daleks were not actually robots as a lot of people imagined, but the last members of a doomed race which had adapted to the corrosive atmosphere of their planet, Skaro, by wearing protective metal armour. The living part of them was, in fact, a slimy, green, brain-sized blob.

The BBC were helpful in lending some of their own Daleks, but the film company's art director, Dennis Ryan, and his team also had to construct some slightly larger fibre-glass models based on drawings loaned by the BBC. The resulting dozen film Daleks were taller, wider and chunkier machines that were much easier to manoeuvre by the operators who stood up in them rather than sitting down. This decision also led to another apocryphal story that Dennis Ryan and not Ray Cusick had been responsible for creating the first Dalek. (See *How I Created The Daleks*.)

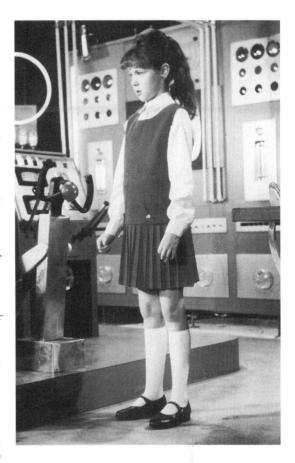

Two of the film Doctor's female companions: Above, Susan (Roberta Tovey) and, opposite, the glamorous Louise (Jill Curzon).

According to Milton Subotsky, he chose Peter Cushing to play the Doctor because he believed his starring roles in the Hammer horror films would be a good selling point to break into the US market where the TV series was then unknown. Milton also decided on the title for the movie, *Dr Who and the Daleks*, and in re-writing Terry Nation's original script opted to give the inventor-Doctor a small London home where he lives and works with his *two* granddaughters, Barbara (Jennie Linden) and Susan (Roberta Tovey). The three of them, plus Barbara's boyfriend, Ian (Roy Castle, who had appeared the previous year with Cushing in *Doctor Terror's House of Horrors*) were then hurled to Skaro in the home-made TARDIS and had to face a life or death battle with the Daleks.

The film was shot in just a month from 8 March to 9 April at Shepperton Studios. Two huge sets were built on what was then the biggest sound stage in Europe: one of the interior of the Dalek city on Skaro and the other the planet's dead forest. The budget for the picture was just £200,000.

Peter Cushing enjoyed the experience immensely. 'It was such a delight to get away from Christopher Lee and his fangs,' he joked. 'For years I had wanted to appear in something that children could see. I knew that lots of them had tried to get in to see the Hammer films because I got letters about it. With *Dr Who and the Daleks* they wouldn't have that problem.

'It was also fascinating to work with the Daleks because until that moment in time all my monsters had been humanoid. We did have a problem with them because of the flashing lights. The director, Gordon Flemyng, didn't realise that the lights flashed when the Daleks were speaking and thought they just went on and off all the time. They had to change some of the script to make sense of a number of scenes.'

When *Dr Who and the Daleks* was released on 24 June that same year, audiences loved the film but the critics hated it. The box-office takings, however, were good enough for Milton Subotsky to take up his option, and he selected Terry Nation's second Dalek story, *World's End* (aka *The Dalek Invasion of Earth*) which had been shown on TV in the run-up to Christmas 1964. Again the title was changed to *The Daleks: Invasion Earth 2150 AD* and in the Doctor's party this time when they travelled forward in time to a devastated London of the future were Susan, a new companion, Louise (Jill Curzon) and a policeman, Tom Campbell (Bernard Cribbins) who had mistakenly stepped into the TARDIS believing it to be a real police box! Here they joined up with some resistance fighters in order to defeat the Daleks who had come to Earth in a vast flying saucer.

Gordon Flemyng was again the director and filming started on 31 January 1966. It was, though, a much less happy experience for Peter.

'I became very ill during the filming and had to stop work,' he recalled. 'In my absence Gordon went on filming around me, but it was very difficult for him, poor man. When I was finally allowed to go back, I was still feeling pretty groggy and I'm afraid Doctor Who was not so lively in that second adventure. Dear Bernard Cribbins tried to keep me smiling when we were filming on location, but it was so cold most of the time. It was quite a relief to get into Shepperton where they had built a bombed-out site in London and half of the Daleks' flying saucer.'

Despite not feeling well, Peter still gave a revealing interview to William Hall of the London *Evening News* on 25 March 1966.

'It was no surprise to me to learn that the first Doctor Who film came into the top twenty box-office hits last year, despite the panning the critics gave it,' he said. 'That's why we've made this sequel and why they are spending almost twice as much money on it . . . I know a lot of people have accused me of lowering my standards in some of the pictures I've done, but I've never felt I'm wasting myself. You have to have a great ego to want to play Hamlet all the time and I just haven't got that ego. Challenge me on this and I'll say, "Well, I've kept working".'

Surprisingly, despite the larger budget, *The Daleks: Invasion Earth 2150 AD* failed to catch on at the box office and fared much less well than its predecessor. Plans that Milton Subotsky had already discussed with Peter for a third film based on Terry Nation's Dalek story *The Chase* were therefore abandoned. But this was not quite the last he heard of the Doctor – or the Daleks.

In 1978, following the huge success of *Star Wars* in which Peter had played the evil Grand Moff Tarkin, Milton Subotsky approached him once again with the idea of co-starring with the current television Doctor, Tom Baker, in a film provisionally entitled *Doctor Who's Greatest Adventure*. This picture – which would have utilised Subotsky's third and final option on the series – was to bring about yet another return for the Daleks, with Peter playing a more advisory role to his younger 'self'. Again this never got beyond the planning stage.

Peter Cushing's experiences as the Doctor did, however, lead to him being offered roles in two other popular sf series, *The Avengers* and *Space: 1999*. In September 1966, a month after the opening of the second Dalek movie, he filmed an episode of *The Avengers* as Paul Beresford, a rich art

Devastated London –
a scene from *The
Daleks: Invasion Earth
2150 AD.*

dilettante who is financing the development of cybernauts in 'Return of the Cybernauts' by Philip Levene. Beresford plans to use the humanoid machines to kidnap a group of influential scientists and comes within an ace of succeeding but for the intrepid pair, John Steed and Emma Peel (Patrick Macnee and Diana Rigg), and suffers a nasty death at the hands of a robot when it runs amok. Interestingly, this episode was screened just a week after another Philip Levene story, 'Who's Who?' Peter was again seen in *The Avengers* in 1976 when he played Von Claus, an eminent specialist in suspended animation in 'The Eagle's Nest' by Brian Clemens. A year earlier in 1975, he had appeared in Gerry and Sylvia Anderson's *Space: 1999* as an anthropologist, Raan, in 'Missing Link' by Edward Di Lorenzo. It also featured the series' star, Commander John Koenig (Martin Landau) who is transported through space and time to the planet Zeno where he falls in love with Raan's daughter, Vana (Joanna Dunham). Shades of *Doctor Who!*

After the death of Helen Cushing on 14 January 1971, it took Peter eleven years to surface publicly, and he longed for the day when he would be reunited with her. He threw himself into work, appearing with Christopher Lee in several more movies, playing Sherlock Holmes in *The Masks of Death* (1984) and what was to be his last picture, *Biggles*, in 1986. He published two volumes of autobiography, *Peter Cushing: An Autobiography* (1986) and *Past Forgetting: Memoirs of the Hammer Years* (1988); and in 1988 he was awarded an OBE for his services to the world of entertainment. (After this, Peter humorously awarded himself the initials MOG – 'Miserable Old Git'!)

In 1993 he was given a surprise eightieth birthday party in Whitstable which was attended by many friends and fellow actors. Among them were Gwen Watford with whom he had co-starred in *The Ghoul* and considered 'a charming person and an actress of the highest order', plus his co-star from the first *Doctor Who* film, Roy Castle, whom he also greatly admired for his fight against cancer.

Sadly, Peter Cushing himself died of prostate cancer on 11 August 1994, and when he was buried in Whitstable eight days later, thousands of friends and fans lined the streets of his home town. Curiously, only one of his obituaries made mention of his contribution to the legend of *Doctor Who* – the *Independent* which said that among his many pictures, 'he is still remembered as the big-screen Time Lord'. Small acknowledgement indeed for the 'heroic role' which he considered among his favourites. It was an omission I feel sure he would be pleased I have put right.

How I Created the Daleks

On 23 September 1994, the following report appeared in several national newspapers under the headline TRAGEDY OF THE DALEK MAN. 'The special effects man who designed the Daleks for TV's *Doctor Who* died after months of starving himself, an inquest heard yesterday. Dennis Ryan, a 53-year-old divorcee, cut himself off from the outside world after being made redundant in 1982 and rarely ventured out from his flat in Lee, south-east London, Southwark Coroners' Court was told. He allowed himself to waste away, refusing to eat properly, wash, or get out of bed for much of the time. Verdict: Death by natural causes.'

In fact, the designer of the Daleks was Raymond P. Cusick of the BBC, who had been allocated £750 to create six Daleks, but because of the costs was only able to run to four built by Shawcraft Models, who

Ray Cusick, the man who designed the Daleks.

had earlier made the TARDIS. Inspired partly by the sight of a pepper pot in the BBC canteen and another suggestion from Terry Nation that they should have a gliding motion, Ray's original drawings took three hours one Friday, and he completed the designs the following Sunday afternoon at home. He realised the Daleks would have to have a human operator, so the basic design was shaped around a man sitting on a tricycle. He initially thought about using midgets to make the machines smaller than humans, but quickly abandoned this idea. The result was a creation of which he was justifiably proud – and following the report of the tragic death of Dennis Ryan, he wrote to the *Daily Telegraph* on 1 October, from his home in Horsham, West Sussex:

> Mr Dennis Ryan whose inquest you reported may have been associated with special effects, but I designed the Daleks for *The Dead Planet* in 1963. The only brief I was given was that they should not show any kind of feet. Their inspiration was a troupe of Russian dancers then playing in London who wore long dresses and had a rolling gait which gave the impression that they had no legs.
>
> Since the programme had a very low budget, I supervised the production of only four Daleks in all. If more were needed for a crowd scene, the black and white images of television meant we could blow up photographs to show more at the back. I was associated with *Doctor Who* for three years until responsibility was transferred in 1966 to another BBC department. Needless to say, I have not shared in the BBC's profits, apart from one small pay-off. But I am still proud of the Daleks!

Another member of the team who worked on the creation of the Daleks was Jack Clayton, who was responsible for the monsters' unforgettable grating voices. He, too, wrote to *The Times* from his home in Saxmundham, Suffolk to set the record straight:

> In 1963 I was in charge of the studio sound in the first series of *Doctor Who* and like the designer, Ray Cusick, I was given freedom to interpret the scripts. He was only told to avoid showing feet; so far as I recall the script it simply described the Dalek voices as 'metallic'.

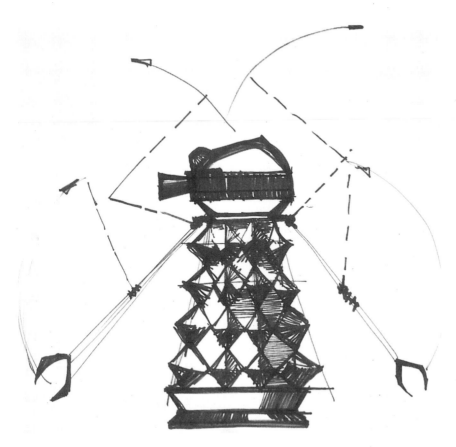

One of Ray Cusick's early sketches made while he was designing the Daleks.

Mr Cusick and I made our preparations separately, and it was only when the production reached the studio that the vision and sound came together. The combination was an instant success and the Daleks made a considerable impact upon the viewers of the day.

The first and most memorable voice of the Daleks was that of actor Peter Hawkins who, with the additional help of the radiophonic sound engineer Brian Hodgson, soon became the most imitated voice in the country. Peter continued to provide the Dalek voices in many of the later productions and his versatile tones were also employed for the Cybermen. Outside of *Doctor Who*, Peter provided voice-overs for a great many animated TV series and even appeared as himself in programmes such as the *Dave Allen Show*.

The Intrepid Clown

? Sprawling Bushy Park which lies near the River Thames between Teddington and Hampton is not perhaps the place one would have expected to find a Time Lord. Yet it was to this oasis of trees and greensward with its Deer Pen and curiously named Leg-of-Mutton Pond, that Patrick Troughton would come regularly to exercise the family's twin labradors, Bill and Ben, especially around the picturesque area known as 'The Woodlands' where a tree is now planted in his memory.

For most of his career, Patrick Troughton avoided publicity like the plague. He once insisted that he never gave interviews, and it was only with considerable persuasion that he agreed to attend *Doctor Who* conventions long after he had given up the role. He believed passionately that an actor's talent was like a magician's art and it was a mistake to give away the secrets of that skill. He wanted to be judged solely on what the public saw of him on the screen. 'People can get very romantic about a part like the Doctor, but it *is* just a job and I'm just a character actor playing a character role,' he once said quite bluntly. (See *What Is There to Say?*)

Yet in October 1982, while working on my first book about the series, I shared a walk with him in Bushy Park where he talked about his three years as the Doctor. A short, blue-eyed man with his shock of hair then turned grey, he lived close by in Hampton but preferred to have our conversation in the park. I have to admit this was something of a disappointment for me as I was dying for a peek at the selection of nostalgic photographs taken during his career, which I knew were stuck up on the wall of his loo! Why *there*? Because as he once said, 'Where better to put them if you want seriously to contemplate what you've done over the years?'

PATRICK TROUGHTON

ACTOR: Patrick Troughton (1920–87)

TIME-SPAN: 1966–9

CHARACTERISTICS: A Chaplinesque figure with an off-beat sense of humour. Always scruffily dressed, he was a zany, whimsical man capable of moments of brilliant improvisation. He was especially ingenious when it came to outwitting adversaries like the Cybermen and the Yeti.

APPEARANCE: His shabby black frock coat was several sizes too big as were his white shirt and baggy trousers. Initially, the Doctor's trousers had a bright orange-and-black check, but these were later changed for a plain black pair. They were invariably held up by a safety pin. Another pin was used to keep his untidy bow tie in place. Early on he wore a tall stove pipe hat over his shaggy brown hair (his own and *not* a wig) and for a time gave added emphasis to his eccentricity by wearing a pair of pixie boots.

One of Patrick Troughton's own photographs of a typical comic moment during the making of *Doctor Who*.

As we walked and the two dogs ran and played around us in the peaceful setting, he said that he was a country person at heart. He was fascinated by wildlife and would have liked to have been a naturalist, except for the fact he was afraid of spiders and snakes. Instead, he was never happier than working in his garden or doing things with his hands.

Dressed in crumpled jeans, a roomy sweater and old suede shoes, Patrick still looked as sprightly and slim as he had done in the sixties. Though not a health fanatic, he never forgot that he had had to have one lung removed because of chain-smoking, and he also watched his diet. Yet despite his desire to protect his privacy, the details of his career prior to joining *Doctor Who* are well documented.

Patrick George Troughton was born in Mill Hill, London, on 25 March 1920 and educated at Bexhill-on-Sea Preparatory School and Mill Hill Public School. 'I did a bit of acting at school, but it was not until I was sixteen that I decided I wanted to become an actor,' he recalled years later. 'I heard a radio programme about Fay Compton and I was interested in what she had to say. The life she described appealed to me and I felt I'd like that kind of life for myself. I actually met her for the first time a few years ago and I told her she was to blame for influencing me into the acting profession.'

He then trained at the Embassy School of Acting in London and in 1939 won a scholarship to Leighton Rollins Studio for Actors at the John Drew Memorial Theatre at East Hampton on Long Island, New York. When the Second World War broke out, Patrick returned home on a Belgian ship which struck an enemy mine and sank just off Portland Bill and reckoned he was lucky to escape with his life. Not deterred by his experience, though, Patrick joined the Royal Navy and saw action on destroyers and on motor torpedo boats based at Great Yarmouth, finally being given his own command after the Allied invasion of Normandy.

After the war, he returned to acting and appeared in repertory at Amersham, played Shakespeare at the Bristol Old Vic, and gave a memorable performance as Hitler in the Gateway production of *Eva Braun* in 1950 which demonstrated his particular skill for character acting. At the same time he began appearing in the new medium of television and was the small screen's first Robin Hood as well as playing Charles Dickens' Quilp in *The Old Curiosity Shop* and co-starring in a number of the early series such as *Dr Finlay's Casebook.*

Patrick was in Ireland filming *The Viking Queen* in 1966 when Sydney Newman offered him the role of the Doctor. 'I have to be quite honest and say that I didn't want to play the part,' he admitted. 'I had a feeling that it had perhaps been done to death and it probably wouldn't last more than six weeks after Billy Hartnell. But they kept pushing the money up so that finally I said, OK, believing it would all be over after a few episodes and it would be just one more job and I'd move on to the next.'

Sydney Newman was delighted at securing Patrick Troughton's signature and quickly informed the press: 'Our problem in choosing the new Doctor Who was very difficult because we have decided to make considerable changes in the personality of the character. We believe we have found exactly the man we wanted.' For his part, Patrick knew his Doctor would have to be very different to that of his predecessor, whose adventures he and his wife Shelagh had watched from the outset. His daughter Jane and two sons David and Michael were then aged between eight and twelve so he felt he should bear them in mind and not make the character too frightening. He said later that if the children had been grown-up, a very different character altogether might have emerged.

The Troughton family all agreed that the Doctor's futuristic adventures were better than the historical ones, and Troughton was pleased to learn from the new script editor, Robert Holmes, that this was to be the emphasis in his stories. He was also interested to discover that Hartnell had become increasingly concerned with the fact that aliens were not necessarily enemies just because they were different, and this became an idea he was keen to pursue.

But what about the new Doctor's appearance? 'We went through a lot of costume ideas,' he recalled with a smile, at the same time paying tribute to the work of the series' costume designer Sandra Reid. 'Sydney Newman, probably aware of my penchant for comedy, suggested I play him like Charlie Chaplin. I thought about blacking up and wearing a huge earring, turban and big grey beard so that no one would recognise me – but the BBC wouldn't hear of it. I also suggested playing him as a tough, wind-jammer captain in full Victorian-style uniform, but when Sydney Newman saw me in this, he shook his head and asked what had happened to the Chaplinesque figure, the "cosmic hobo". And that was it. We went to the costumers and sorted out some things. I found this tall black hat that Mr Quilp might have worn and with the recorder that was my Doctor sorted.'

The result was a somewhat comical figure – 'a bit like Billy Hartnell as a tramp!' Troughton later joked – complete with the stove-pipe hat that was to prove the first of several eccentric items of headgear he would wear during the series. Patrick also added to his props a packet of jelly baby sweets to dispense during his adventures. Interestingly, while Tom Baker's Doctor is most associated with jelly babies, Troughton actually introduced this novelty in his very first story, the explosive *Power of the Daleks* by David Whitaker which went out most appropriately on Bonfire Night, 5 November 1966.

Patrick confessed later that he tried hard to master the recorder during his three years in the series – using it as a means of signifying the Doctor's mood – and was proud of the fact that by playing it he had apparently instigated an upsurge of interest in the instrument among children. It also used to encourage him into doing outrageous things on set, he said, and sometimes the director had to deliberately hide it away. This combination of the recorder, the character's whimsical nature and his habit of leading his companions into adventures made him seem very much like a contemporary Pied Piper.

Patrick also brought to the role his well-honed skills of mime and character observation. Throughout his career, he always prided himself on 'thinking' himself into a part so that no matter how fantastic that person might be, he *believed* in it. As one of his producers, Peter Bryant, said at the time, 'Pat just feels there *is* a Doctor Who – and as long as he feels this, he will jolly well *be* him.'

In the beginning, Troughton played the Doctor in a very clownish way, but mellowed as the series progressed. He was clearly inventing all the time, and putting new things into the role as he went along. Although always off-beat, Pat's Doctor remained essentially human-like.

The Second Doctor always tried to see the funny side in any situation – especially when confronting the various monsters which are now seen as a particular feature of his era in the series: the Yeti, the Krotons, Ice Warriors, and most of all, the Cybermen whom he confronted on no less than four occasions.

Three actors dressing in their Cybermen outfits during filming of *The Invasion* (1968) near St Paul's Cathedral in London.

'I suppose you could say they were my particular enemy,' he reflected. 'I must admit I thought the idea of a race of automatons was quite clever, although I always had difficulty in telling which one was speaking because you had to keep an eye on the one with its mouth-flap open. I finally cracked the problem by getting the actor who was speaking to shift an arm or stoop forward slightly so that I knew which way to turn.' (See *Cyberdad and the Cybermen*.)

Because of the number of monsters in the series, Patrick became full of admiration for the actors who were inside the often very hot and claustrophobic skins. He liked several of the creatures, but had a particular soft spot for the Yeti because he thought the whole idea was so good and the costumes were 'so cuddly!'

The Yeti story, *The Abominable Snowmen* by Mervyn Halsman and Henry Lincoln, was filmed primarily at Nant Ffrancon Pass in Snowdonia during September 1967 and some local people in that part of Wales can still recall the fun of having the Doctor, camera crew and cast on location for a week – especially the four actors who played the Yeti, Reg Whitehead, Richard Kerley, Tony Harwood and John Hogan.

To begin with, though, the shoot had all the makings of a nightmare for director Gerry Blake because of high winds and rain. 'We knew we couldn't go down to Surrey and pretend it was Tibet, that would have looked awful,' he said in an interview later. 'But we hadn't bargained for the bad weather that hit us in Wales and straight away we lost a couple of days' filming.'

Reg Whitehead also remembers the week vividly. 'The rain made the place very muddy and slippery so that we were falling about all over the place whenever we moved because we couldn't see a thing from inside the fur. Mind you, we had the laugh on those who made fun of us because we were as warm as toast and very comfortable, while everyone else was getting their balls frozen off!'

The suits were made by Martin Baugh of the BBC costume department with the fur stretched across a frame of bamboo canes worn on the actors' shoulders. The faces had no features and the hands and feet were made of thick rubber. All four Yeti towered over their human protagonists and had a gimmick which fans latched on to as soon as they appeared on the screen: a silver control sphere in the chest which gave out a bleeping sound as easy for children to imitate as the Daleks' 'Ex-ter-min-ate! Ex-ter-min-ate!'

Patrick Troughton was particularly struck at the way youngsters took to the hulking creatures and wherever the cast and crew went they would always be followed by a gang of children who stared at the Yeti and would even stroke them if they could get close enough. Such, indeed, was the affection in which the creatures were held, that photographs of Reg Whitehead and his colleagues taken at Nant Ffrancon are still to be seen in the scrapbooks of local *Doctor Who* fans who are now middle-aged men and women.

Although after the two lost days Patrick found shooting *The Abominable Snowmen* 'rather like jumping on a running bus', it was still great fun. He especially remembered one occasion when Gerry Blake had a little joke at the expense of some people who turned up to watch the filming.

'While we were shooting, one of them asked, tongue-in-cheek, if we were making a film. Gerry overheard this and looked at us with a grin. "Watch this!" he said. He then put on this wonderful Hollywood director's voice and shouted to the crew, "No, no! I want that mountain moved seven inches to the *left!*" The props lads immediately realised what he was up to and grabbed some shovels. "OK, guvnor," they said. Before we all fell about laughing, we heard the same person gasp, "Oh, bloody hell, they're going to move our mountain!"'

There was never any doubt from the reactions of the public that the Yeti would return in another story which they duly did in *The Web of Fear* by Haisman and Lincoln in February 1968 when they were made rather nastier with glowing eyes and a gun which sprayed their victims with an asphyxiating web. These new versions quickly earned the nickname among the cast of 'Angry Teddy Bears'. Sadly, a third adventure in which the snowmen were to find their way to a remote Scottish castle to wreak havoc was never made.

Despite the violence exhibited by many of his adversaries, Troughton's Doctor never engaged in physical combat himself. His sharpest weapon was his mind and there was clearly a superior intelligence behind the comic mask. The apparent fool was not a man to be trifled with, as many an enemy discovered.

Patrick believed that it was Gerry Davis and Kit Pedler who dreamed up the concept of the Doctor regenerating into a completely new body to explain the change-over from William Hartnell. His ground-breaking debut story was originally to have been called *The Destiny of Doctor Who*, but was changed to *The Power of the Daleks* to reassure viewers that even if there was a new human star, the series' most popular villains *were* returning. Patrick himself remembered settling into the role of the Doctor with comparative ease, helped initially by Ben and Polly, the two companions he inherited from his predecessor played by Michael Craze and Anneke Wills.

'It wasn't easy stepping into someone else's shoes, but they were marvellous to me,' he said. 'For the first few weeks before we started filming, the three of us spent time together in various pubs getting to know each other. On the first day of shooting, they came on to the set wearing t-shirts with the words, "Come Back, Bill Hartnell" and we all just cracked up.'

His partnership with the trio who took over from Craze and Wills shortly afterwards was to prove even more successful. The three were Frazer Hines, playing the Scottish lad, Jamie McCrimmon (1966–9); the highly intelligent Zoe Herriott played by Wendy Padbury (1968–9); and Deborah Watling as the pretty but rather naive Victoria Waterfield (1967–8). I first met Debbie, the daughter of actor Jack Watling (who himself appeared in the series as Professor Travers in *The Abominable Snowmen*) when I was a newspaper reporter in her home town of Loughton in Essex – we all three judged a competition for children at the local cinema – and she later proved a valuable source of stories about the making of *Doctor Who*. Not a few of them proved to be about practical jokes perpetrated at her own expense!

Patrick Troughton always remembered that Deborah had to put up with a lot of teasing. 'I remember once we were in the TARDIS waiting for our cue. We were standing behind Debbie and just before we got the cue, Frazer and I whipped down her pants and then opened the door and walked out. She was left behind giggling, trying to struggle into her pants and get on to the set! On another occasion we were rehearsing in this church hall and unknown to her, Frazer had undone her kilt. As soon as she got up it fell off and, suspecting it was one or another of us, she began chasing us around the hall. Just at that moment, the vicar walked in. Even as she was, Debbie stopped and curtsied to him and we fell about.'

Despite such indignities, Debbie had the highest regard for her co-star. She found him exceedingly charming. And if ever he was the centre of a group of actors around a bar, she said, he would be telling the dirtiest jokes.

Waiting for a break in the rain during filming of *The Krotons* (1968) in a Dorking slate quarry.

'He was always playing pranks,' she said. 'I remember one occasion when he was supposed to be producing the coloured handkerchief from his pocket, and instead pulled out a pair of lady's knickers. The whole production team just roared and looked at me. It didn't matter how much I protested that they weren't mine, no one believed it!'

Patrick was also the one who answered the question then on every viewer's lips – did Jamie wear anything under his kilt. 'Yes. He wore a pair of khaki shorts.'

His admiration for all three actors remained undiminished. 'I was very lucky having Frazer Hines, Deborah Watling and Wendy Padbury with me for so long. Somehow I always used to find myself running with Frazer and Debbie and as I was the Doctor I felt I should run faster than them. But they were young and I was old and it was difficult.'

One of the stories which most amused Patrick was *The Krotons* by Robert Holmes screened at Christmas 1968. The scenes with the Kroton monsters had been shot the previous month in a slate quarry near Dorking. As Robert Holmes explained, 'The Krotons were supposed to be big, powerful and very threatening crystalline creatures that could be generated from chemicals in a matter of moments – instead they looked like angry egg boxes.'

'They were hysterical,' Patrick Troughton recalled. 'One of them was supposed to be chasing Frazer and me, roaring its head off. Well, we set off across the quarry but all the Kroton did was to make a sound like a muffled cough and fall over! It had to be helped around like an old man after that – the poor sod inside [Robert La Bassiere] just couldn't breathe, let alone move it!'

Energy in plenty was something that Patrick Troughton said he needed while filming *Doctor Who* which he described as being rather like working for a repertory company.

'The show was on every Saturday night of the year except in August,' he explained, 'and we often filmed at weekends which meant it was a seven-day-a-week job just like in rep. We only had a few days to learn the scripts and rehearse before we were on. It was absolutely exhausting and after three years I knew I had to get out. There was a real danger of becoming schizophrenic about the whole thing.'

Like his predecessor, Patrick sensed he was getting rather edgy at rehearsals and, when filming, becoming angry at small things. He had several arguments with the producer and directors and realised he was in danger of being seen as 'a monster like some of those I was up against in the stories'. Initially, he wanted to leave the series after making *The Mind Robber* by Peter Ling in the autumn of 1968, but being only too well aware of the problems that there had been in finding him as a replacement for William Hartnell, agreed to stay until a new Doctor had been chosen the following spring.

When Patrick Troughton left *Doctor Who*, his mastery of character acting meant that he was not out of work for long. But such was his affection for the series that he accepted invitations to return in a trio of subsequent stories, *The Three Doctors* in 1972, the twentieth anniversary special; *The Five Doctors* in 1983; and *The Two Doctors* in 1984. In the first of these, he appeared with William Hartnell and his own successor Jon Pertwee, in a story written by Bob Baker and Dave Martin that was to have been entitled *The Black Hole*.

'It was lovely working with Jon and we developed quite a rapport,' he said. 'But poor Billy was a bit ga-ga, although it was nice to have him along.'

Patrick hugely enjoyed making *The Five Doctors* by Terrance Dicks although the different make-up on his hair left many fans convinced he must have worn a wig during his three years in the role – a fact which he vigorously denied. Filming *The Two Doctors* by Robert Holmes (which also began its script life as *The Kraglon Inheritance*) with Colin Baker entailed location work in Seville, Spain in August 1984. The heat was terrific, but fortunately there was a swimming pool close to hand which proved a godsend when things went wrong.

'There was a bit of a cock-up with the make-up and wigs and so forth which didn't arrive until we got there,' Patrick recalled later. 'So we couldn't shoot a scene. So we were paid to just lie around in the sun by the hotel pool and learn our lines until they got some fresh eyebrows and hair through.'

The 'fearsome' Kroton which kept falling over.

Patrick also remembered returning home from location shooting one night to find there was no food available and so he made do with a packet of wine gums and the contents of a hip flask. The following morning, he said, he woke up not surprisingly with a touch of 'Spanish tummy'.

For a man who so stubbornly resisted public appearances throughout much of his career, it was a tragedy that his death was to occur while doing just that. Once he had made the decision to attend conventions in the early eighties, any that he went to in Britain or America received his full co-operation. Not for him hours in the hospitality suites so beloved by certain stars, but instead he could often be found in the corner of a foyer lounge where he would chat and sign autographs for all-comers.

Patrick was attending an American *Doctor Who* convention at Columbus in Georgia when he was found lying on the floor of his hotel room on the morning of Saturday 28 March 1987. He was rushed to hospital but was found to have died of a heart attack. After cremation his ashes were flown back to London where his loss was as deeply felt by the acting profession as by fans of *Doctor Who*. He was 67.

Curiously, his final television appearance filmed just before the convention was in a role that brought back memories of the Doctor. He starred in the ITV series *Supergran*, televised on 31 May 1987, playing the Great Sporran of the Isles, a comic figure wearing an outrageous hat, frock coat, baggy trousers and a long grey beard of the kind he had been denied in *Doctor Who*. The story was all about a ghost hunt in a Scottish castle and director Tony Kysh recalled later, 'He was just as full of energy and leaping about like an eighteen-year-old as he had been in *Doctor Who*.' Even one of his lines harked back to the role for which he will always be remembered: ' *Who* would believe it?'

'What Is There to Say?'

Patrick Troughton became renowned after leaving *Doctor Who* for claiming to remember very little about the series during the time that he was in it. In fact, this was just another aspect of this private and elusive man, and when he did become more public about his role as the Doctor in the eighties he would invariably turn up at conventions in his familiar costume and duck and dive his way around questions with all the charm and *élan* of a politician. 'They don't want to see *me*,' he once said, a grin from ear to ear, 'they want to see Doctor Who!'

These appearances were, in fact, just another performance from his amazing repertoire, and to pull together the facts about his three years in the series has been very much a case of mining nuggets of information from the years between 1966 until his death as all those writers and fans who have tried have discovered.

He treated me to a typical example of his roguish sense of fun in 1982 when I first made contact with him and he replied with the following letter:

Dear Peter Haining,

There's very little to tell you I'm afraid – it's so very long ago that I played the part – and I've played so many different parts in the last forty years.

Q. *'How did I feel about playing the part?'*

A. To begin with I thought it would last about six weeks more after Billy Hartnell. But my contribution lasted three years as it turned out – and that was a show every Saturday each year except for August. They only do a few each year now, so it was very hard work. Nevertheless, it was the happiest time of my professional life – except for a play which I have just done with Gwen Watford on BBC TV. [*Reluctant Chickens* screened in 1983.]

Q. *'Why is Doctor Who such a continuing success?'*

A. Because new children keep on being born.

Q. *'What was the impact of the series on my career?'*

A. None. Luckily I got out in time before I was too typecast.

Q. *'Any anecdotes?'*

A. None you could print in a children's book!

Cyberdad and the Cybermen

The Cybermen, second only in popularity to the Daleks in *Doctor Who*, were created jointly by the scriptwriters Gerry Davis and Kit Pedler and costume designer Sandra Wise. They first appeared in *The Tenth Planet*, the final adventure of the first Doctor, but established their enduring infamy during Patrick Troughton's tenure as the time traveller.

Gerry Davis, who lived in Elklund Place in Venice, California until his tragic death from stomach cancer in 1991, wrote to me several letters during the eighties about the creation of these merciless robot killers which earned him the nickname 'Cyberdad' from American fans of the series. Initially a newspaper reporter in Hastings, Gerry had been a merchant seaman for four years and then a scriptwriter on Canadian radio before his path crossed that of Sydney Newman at the National Film Board of Canada. He returned to England in 1966, where he again met up with Newman and was subsequently recruited as script editor of *Doctor Who*.

'I wanted to inject the science back into the series,' Gerry said. 'Hartnell's Doctor had a lot of adventures in the past and it seemed time to break new ground with some sci-fi themes. So I got in touch with a number of the leading popular scientists including Alex Comfort, Patrick Moore and Christopher Pedler to see if they had any ideas for the series. Kit Pedler, who was a medical doctor and surgeon at London University and an sf fan into the bargain, rose to the challenge brilliantly.'

Pedler had, in fact, already been involved in television, designing the monster which took over Westminster Abbey in *The Quatermass Experiment*. During one of their meetings, Pedler admitted to Gerry that his greatest fear was that medicine would one day become dehumanised. There were now so many 'spare parts' being provided for patients, that he believed there was a real danger of human beings turning into robots.

'I saw the idea at once,' said Gerry. 'Men with everything replaced by cybernetics, lacking all human feelings and invulnerable to heat or cold. They would be the ultimate monsters, creatures driven solely by the desire for power. I think it is true to say we both came up with the name at the same moment . . . Cybermen.'

Together, Gerry and Kit worked out the plot of an adventure for the Doctor battling with the Cybermen and a sketch of what one might

Wookey Hole Caves in Somerset was another location in which the Cybermen appeared – this time in *Revenge of the Cybermen* filmed in 1974.

look like, which they handed to Sandra Wise. Although the first Cybermen Sandra created were very rudimentary, the 'look' she produced set the basic pattern which was revised several times by later designers on the series.

Each of Sandra Reid's original Cybermen for *The Tenth Planet* was swathed in a body stocking from head to foot, with three gauze-covered holes for the eyes and mouth. Over this went a polythene suit, ribbed with metal rings and supports to add rigidity. Clamped to the chest of each was a life-support unit fitted with batteries to provide flashing lights, and beneath this a Cyber-gun shaped like a small camera which fired laser beams. On their heads the Cybermen wore a metal skull cap attached to the 'headlamps' and 'jug-handle' supports which had to be made secure by the use of lots of sticky-tape! The outfits were completed with ordinary wellington boots which had been painted silver.

Reg Whitehead, who played one of the early Cybermen, recalled later: 'The costumes were terribly heavy and hot to wear, and several people actually fainted under the hot studio lights. Only by taking off the gloves could some cool air be let into the suits.'

The actor also remembered when one of the original Cybermen was given his first public airing in a street market not far from the studios in Shepherds Bush. 'It was actually a bit of an anti-climax, because no one ran away screaming in terror. One of the stall-holders even laughed and said he thought the costume must be part of an advertising campaign for a new kitchen cleaner!'

However, the impact of the Cybermen on viewers of *Doctor Who* was quite the reverse. When some scenes for a later story, *The Return of the Cybermen* (retitled *The Invasion* before being shown) were filmed in Queen Victoria Street in the shadow of St Paul's Cathedral in September 1968, hundreds of sightseers crowded around the landmark to watch the actors and crew at work. The production team took fewer risks of being disturbed in November 1974 when they were filming *Revenge of the Cybermen* by using the Wookey Hole Caves in Somerset as a stand-in for the inhospitable world of the planet Voga – although it was not until the cast and crew were on site that they learned the caves were allegedly cursed.

Peter Bryant who directed this story featuring Tom Baker's doctor remembered the weird things that happened very well. 'In one of the caves there is a rock formation that looks like a witch – it's actually called the Witch of Wookey Hole – and we were told by one of the people working there not to make fun of it. Well, a couple of the technicians thought it would be funny to dress the rock up while no one was looking and used an old cape and a broom. That same day, one of the cameramen fell off a rock and broke his leg, and Liz Sladen fell into the water and started to get dragged under by the current. The stunt guy, Terry Walsh, happened to be near by and jumped in and saved her, but he was ill for some time after that. We had obviously brought the curse to life and I was pretty glad when we finished filming without any more incidents!'

The second of the Cybermen stories, *Tomb of the Cybermen* made in June 1967, heralded the arrival of another Davis-Pedler invention: the Cybermats; small, vicious, bug-like silver creatures. They were actually radio-controlled models – the first to be used in the BBC studios at Lime Grove – and when shooting began, they suddenly ran amok around the set. It was not until considerable investigation had been carried out that it was discovered the floor manager's headset was on the same frequency as the Cybermats and any signals to him were interacting with the models!

Gerry Davis left *Doctor Who* as script editor in 1967, and later moved to America where he worked on a number of movies including *The Countdown* and TV series such as *The Bionic Woman* and *Captain Power and the Soldiers of the Future*. He was, though, twice more linked with the series. In the early eighties he proposed an outline for *Genesis of the Cybermen* which was inexplicably rejected, and then in 1990 formed a partnership with Terry Nation in an abortive attempt to secure the rights from the BBC to independently produce a new series of *Doctor Who* stories. Sadly, his partner in creating the Cybermen, Kit Pedler, died in 1981.

Gerry himself retained an admiration for the series right until his own death. 'I don't think I'll ever lose my affection for *Doctor Who* and especially the Cybermen,' the man they called Cyberdad told me in one of his last letters in 1989. 'They were both certainly a big influence on my career.'

The Man of Speed

![?] The vehicle being driven alongside the River Thames past Barnes Bridge looked, at first glance, just like a small hovercraft. Passers-by might have been forgiven for expecting the machine with its swept-back cockpit and graceful fins to take to the water as effortlessly as, instead, it turned into Barnes High Street. At the wheel of the vehicle, his craggy face creased in a familiar grin, sat Jon Pertwee, remembered today as the 'gadget Doctor' because of his love of speed and powerful machines which he drove regularly throughout the series. He was also the only Doctor in the series who spent his entire tenure based on Earth.

'The Whomobile was probably the most revolutionary vehicle ever made for the series,' he was quoted proudly as saying in 1979. 'It looked just like a flying saucer.'

By a curious, if perhaps typical quirk of bureaucracy, this two-seater vehicle, registration number WVO 2M, was actually classified by the Road Licensing Department as an *invalid tricycle*. Yet having ridden in it with Jon, I can assure anyone that it would have seen off any invalid carriage with its top speed of 100 mph! Nor can many other similar vehicles have contained such an array of instrumentation including a telephone, stereo system, television, mock-up computer and a button (guaranteed to make any passenger feel a little uneasy) marked 'Ejector Seat'. But when Jon first presented the vehicle to the licensing authority in 1973, the civil servants found the combination of futuristic car, part spaceship and part hovercraft, impossible to categorise under the existing guidelines and opted instead for the unlikely designation of invalid carriage.

JON PERTWEE

ACTOR: Jon Pertwee (1919–96)

TIME-SPAN: 1970–74

CHARACTERISTICS: A flamboyant and dashing man of action, though always meticulous and precise. Occasionally camp but always charismatic, he was a scientist to the core and dedicated to protecting Earth against alien invaders. The Doctor was addicted to gadgets and spectacular forms of transport such as the vintage roadster, Bessie, and his car of the future, the Whomobile.

APPEARANCE: Initially he wore a flowing, red satin-lined cape over a black velvet smoking jacket. The outfit was completed with a ruffled shirt and neckties of varying colours. Later, the Doctor sported a red jacket with a purple-lined cloak and occasionally wore his shirts open at the neck. He made several changes to the colour scheme of this outfit during the later stories. His fair hair was always immaculately coiffured.

The unmistakable shock of hair reveals that it is Jon Pertwee at the wheel of the Whomobile.

Jon was more amused than angry at this insult to his pride and joy, and thereafter delighted in showing off the car around the streets of Barnes where he lived with his wife, Ingeborg, in an imposing town house on Castelnau full of Elizabethan furniture (bought because of his love of the Tudor period). He was stopped by the police on a number of occasions – but it was almost always so that the officer could have a look at the vehicle or perhaps get the third Doctor's autograph for a son or daughter.

'It happened time and again,' he recalled. 'I'd be driving along and a police car would pull me over. Once I'd opened the roof, they'd realise at once who I was. I always used to tell them that the car met all the legal requirements, but there was one officer who looked at me and shook his head. "I'm sorry, sir, but you still can't drive a hovercraft on the road." And I then had to get the chap to bend down and look under the rubber skirt and convince himself that it *did* have wheels!'

Pure chance played a part in Jon becoming so inextricably linked with the Whomobile. In January 1973, he performed the opening ceremony at a new Ford Main Dealers in Nottingham. On display was a specially customised Ford Black Widow, all gleaming paint and chrome. Jon could not take his eyes off it, and introduced himself to the owner, Peter Farries, the chairman of the Nottingham Drag and Custom Club.

'It just suddenly occurred to me while we were talking,' Jon explained. 'I asked Peter if he could make *me* a car like it. I told him I wanted it to look like something from outer space that could fly or go underwater or whatever. It also had to be street legal. He loved the idea and within a couple of minutes had sketched out the vehicle almost exactly as it turned out.'

Building the fourteen-foot-long by seven-foot-wide three-wheeler which would be known originally as 'Alien' took much of that summer. The vehicle consisted primarily of a Bond three-wheeler front end and Hillman Imp rear, with the driver's compartment made from a steel box to provide maximum protection in the event of an accident. The engine was an aluminium 975 cc Imp Sports Unit and the arrangement of the suspension unit and the three wheel/tyre combination made braking unnecessary when cornering. The glass fibre body was moulded in two pieces and painted in silver and red metalflake paint together with twenty coats of lacquer. Around the outside of the body was an eight-inch deep rubber skirt. The cockpit cover had a split-screen window which hinged forward to allow access.

The finishing touches to the vehicle were provided by the four Lucas Silver Sabre spotlights on the front and no fewer than twenty-four twinkle lights which flashed when the car braked. Inside, the two seats were upholstered with air-vented black vinyl and a combination of metal, wood and plastic had been used to give the console a most impressive appearance.

The 'Alien', of which a delighted Jon took delivery in September 1973, weighed just fourteen hundredweight and with its aerodynamic styling could reach almost 100 mph.

'It was a beautiful car – it handled well and the engine was very responsive,' said Jon. 'The only problem I ever had was at top speed or in high wind, when the nose had a tendency to lift up. We solved this by putting some sandbags in the front!'

The Whomobile made its debut in *Invasion of the Dinosaurs* (January 1974), having been hastily written in by the scriptwriter, Malcolm Hulke. 'To get used to the car, I drove it to several of the locations we used in central London,' Jon explained. 'Of course, the car turned heads wherever it went, and I remember that as I was going through Piccadilly, a group of tourists passing by in a car couldn't take their eyes off me and drove straight into the back of a bus. I stopped to make sure they were all right – but they were much more interested in the "Alien" than in any damage that had been done to their car!'

In fact, wherever Jon went at that time in the car, he found himself a focal point of attention. But he became increasingly aware of the number of near accidents he was causing as people were staring at him and not looking where they were going, so he decided to have the car taken to locations on a low-loader and confine himself to taking it out of his garage to drive around Barnes only at weekends. Although the Whomobile was only one of many vehicles he drove both in the series and during his lifetime – ranging from a 50 cc Honda commuter bike to a supercharged 1.5 litre Bugatti – it remained one of his favourites even after he later parted with it in an act of great generosity to a *Doctor Who* fan who had suffered a terrible family trauma.

It was perhaps fated that Jon Pertwee should succeed Patrick Troughton as *Doctor Who*. For like Troughton, he had served in the Navy as an officer during the Second World War and had an amazing escape from death when he was among a party of 16 going ashore from HMS *Hood* when it was sunk by the *Bismarck*. The paths of the two men crossed on several occasions during that time and Jon had early evidence of his friend's streak of eccentricity which he would later bring to the role of the Doctor.

'He had a strong dislike of the standard issue tin hats that the Navy made the people on motor torpedo-boats wear,' said Jon. 'So instead he wore this old family tea cosy on his head. It was a gaudy-looking thing and must have annoyed his Commanding Officer no end – but he still went on wearing it!'

The Navy was, in fact, to play a considerable part in the life of John Devon Roland Pertwee. Born on 7 July 1919, in Chelsea, London, he was the son of the famous playwright and actor Roland Pertwee (the name is derived from the French Perthuis de Laillavault). His childhood, though, was not a happy one.

'My mother and father parted just after I was born, and my father was rather wrapped up in himself and his own life. I was the youngest of three brothers and always felt a bit left out. It was years before I learned the story of my mother's affair and how my father had found out about it. He told her she could get out and he would bring the children up. She went off with her lover and Dad got custody. I didn't actually see my mother again until I was fifteen.

'I became a great rebel,' Jon continued. 'I used to fly off into terrible tempers and I was very uncontrolled and intolerant. I still am terribly intolerant of fools and people who are rude to me, and I admit I am a bit irascible. I believe all of it is due to my upbringing and being very much a lone wolf.'

Notwithstanding all this upheaval, a career in showbusiness seemed inevitable, a fact which Jon himself admitted. 'Because it was the family business I never had a struggle to join in – I took it for granted, which is maybe why I've never taken it seriously enough.'

He was educated at several boarding schools, all remembered by him for the amount of bullying he suffered. 'I wanted to study drama and music and I was always being kicked out to play games. I wasn't a poofter – it was just that I was different and wanted to be an actor.'

Jon did, though, recall one happy moment which was to signal the beginning of his lifelong fascination with speed. 'I was at this co-educational boarding school when I bought a 250 cc SOS trials motorcycle for the princely sum of five pounds. They asked me if I had a licence and insurance, and I said, "Certainly." Of course, I had neither and when I arrived at a T-junction I went straight over the opposite wall into a vicar's garden. "Well done!" he said. "You're just in time for tea!"'

When he was eighteen, Jon joined RADA where he again made an inauspicious start to his intended career by being told he was incompetent and expelled with the message that he should forget all about a career in showbusiness. His optimism undaunted, though, he found work in a travelling theatre company, a circus (where he rode a motorcycle on the Wall of Death), followed by occasional jobs in the theatre and on radio. During this time, he frequently told himself that if he could not make it as an actor then he would like to be a criminologist! Jon was also pursuing his love of speed and bought his first car – a Bullnose Morris Cowley. In the late thirties, he even entered a number of races at Goodwood where he demonstrated a real aptitude for the high-speed sport. Whether he might have made the grade as a racing driver, however, became immaterial when the war broke out and he instead found himself in the RNVR (Royal Naval Volunteer Reserve).

Towards the end of his naval career, Jon joined the broadcasting section of the service where he met Lieutenant Eric Barker and began the radio career which would lead to the two series that made him a household name: *Waterlogged Spa* and *The Navy Lark*. In the latter, he drew freely on his days of service in playing such diverse characters as Commander High-Price, the Norwegian Seaman Svenson and Robin Fly the burglar from Plymouth Barracks. It was, though, as the anonymous Postman that he

Jon Pertwee's Doctor
had no great affection
for the Daleks,
despite this cheerful
photograph taken
with producer
Barry Letts.

caught the nation's ear with a catch-phrase that was soon being repeated all over the country in the fifties: 'What does it matter what you do as long as you tear 'em up?' Jon appeared in *The Navy Lark* for a total of eighteen years and was always proud of the fact that it was the longest-running comedy show in the world.

Sometimes compared to Danny Kaye at this period of his life because of his blond good looks, Jon continued to work in the theatre (enjoying a particular success in *A Funny Thing Happened on the Way to the Forum* with Frankie Howerd) on television and in several of the *Carry On* films. What has since been seen as the decisive moment in his career occurred in 1969 when he was offered the part of the Doctor.

'One day early in 1969 while I was recording *The Navy Lark*, one of the actors, Tenniel Evans, said to me, "Pat Troughton is leaving *Doctor Who* – why don't you put yourself up for the part? I think you would be very good." I thought the idea was ridiculous because although I have always been a bit eccentric in my life and the roles I played, I was still considered by most people to be a light comedian. My agent Richard Stone didn't think it was a very good idea, either, but still decided to get in touch with the BBC. Much to his amazement and mine they already had my name on their short list. It was really weird.'

Jon had watched a few of William Hartnell's *Doctor Who* stories in which his first wife Jean Marsh had appeared, but became more aware of the programme when his former naval companion was in the role because his children, son Sean and daughter Dariel, were great fans. It gave him an idea of how he wanted to approach the role.

'I thought that towards the end of his time in the show, Pat had gone a bit over the top,' said Jon. 'All that stuff with the recorder and the clowning was something I did not want to repeat. I felt there was a chance to reach older viewers by playing the part straight. I wanted to get more science into the stories and I was also keen to include my love for motorcycles, cars, speedboats and all sorts of gadgetry. I also wanted to introduce the use of the martial art Aiki-do. In a sentence, I wanted something for everybody.'

However, on joining the *Doctor Who* team, Jon learned that one of the original reasons for his name being on the list was because the BBC wanted the new Doctor to be a comedian who could sing and play the guitar and do a whole range of voices. In a word, play the Doctor as a minstrel. After a great deal of discussion with the producer, Peter Bryant,

The Doctor's great friend, the Brigadier (Nicholas Courtney).

Jon got his wish and created a character who to some older fans is still regarded as the 'definitive Doctor'.

As to his costume, Jon saw himself in a high-necked, black Nehru-style suit, but this was ruled out. Instead, for his first press call and encouraged to dress as he liked, he wore an old Inverness cape that had belonged to his grandfather, a velvet smoking jacket of his own, and one of the latest frilly shirts by Mr Fish, then one of the leading male fashion houses in London. This outfit proved the model for the Pertwee Doctor costume which was later specially made for him by the Savile Row tailor, Arthur Davey.

Jon did not have to wait long to introduce a vehicle into the series, albeit a veteran rather than a racing car. This was Bessie, a yellow-coloured Edwardian car which was provided for him by Brigadier Lethbridge-Stewart (Nicholas Courtney) when he joined UNIT (United Nations International Taskforce, whose mission was to defeat invasion attempts) as a scientific adviser. Like the Whomobile, Bessie now has an enduring place in the history of *Doctor Who*.

The idea of introducing the Roadster was the first of several that Jon had for the series. He had read all about a company named Siva Ltd of Blandford in Dorset making the limited edition vehicles, and suggested using one to Peter Bryant in his Earth-bound adventures now that the TARDIS was out of operation for the time being. An order was placed for a four-seater Roadster which arrived in time to appear in his second adventure, *The Silurians*, also written by Malcolm Hulke. It remained right through Jon's time as the Doctor. It has subsequently been seen in Tom Baker's debut story, *Robot* (1974) and the Sylvester McCoy episode *Battlefield* (1989).

Bessie was basically a kit car which fitted directly on to an unmodified E93A Ford chassis of the kind used by the motor company in the common Popular, Prefect and Anglia models. To those who chose to make a Roadster themselves – or its equally popular two-seater version – the manufacturers claimed the whole process from removing the Ford body to driving away the vehicle could be achieved in under a month of spare-time working!

Once the Ford bodywork had been dismantled in pieces (wings, bonnet, boot, etc.), the one-piece glass fibre Tourer body, complete with front and back seats of leather cloth over foam cushioning, was ready to be slid into position over the steering column. This could then be bolted directly on to the chassis as was commonplace in the manufacturing of cars in the fifties. Next the fuel tank had to be fitted into its new position, a new 105E Ford Popular radiator fixed at the front of the engine, and the running boards and mudguards added. With the wiring in place, the dashboard and front and rear lights could be attached. The final touch was the simulated artillery wheels bolted to the original hub caps. The basic cost of the kit was a remarkable £160, although the *Doctor Who* production team ordered a number of extras including the coach lamps, hood and side curtains, interior carpets, screen and bonnet straps, bulb horns and a luggage trunk which took the total cost to just £342.

Jon admitted to being very excited when he travelled down to Dorset to take possession of Bessie – but as a speed-lover, he very quickly found that she was not at all like a sports car.

'The car only had an eight horsepower engine, and I over-revved it several times until it blew up,' he recalls. 'The BBC got me another one but this blew up, too. After that we had to go for a bigger, ten horsepower engine which rather unbalanced the car. We had some hairy moments keeping her going!'

Among these 'hairy moments' was an accident during the filming of *Inferno* by Don Houghton (1970) when Bessie accidentally caught the leg of a stunt man jumping out of her way and gashed his shin, and in *The Time Monster* by Robert Sloman (1972) when the car was being filmed down a country lane too narrow to carry a cameraman. A moviecam was fixed to the side of Bessie and the Doctor with his then companion, the mini-skirted, scatterbrained Jo Grant (played by Katy Manning, 1971–3) drove off. When the sequence was completed, Jon suddenly realised he had no idea where they were. It took an anxious search party quite a while to locate the missing Doctor and his motor car.

Although Bessie was invariably seen on the screen bearing the number WHO 1, the BBC had been unable to secure this registration for the vehicle (its actual number was MTR 5) and so it could only be shown in these false plates on private property. Whenever Jon was seen at the wheel on public roads he was always filmed from a distance and at such an angle that the number could not be seen.

The Roadster was also provided with a number of special effects including the 'Super-Drive', an anti-theft device, and a radio control unit. Although this unit was seen apparently working most effectively on several occasions in the series, the effect was actually achieved in the simplest possible way – a couple of prop men pushing the vehicle out of view of the camera and another crouched down under the steering wheel manipulating it at the base! (Curiously, despite the popularity of Bessie and the Whomobile, none of the toy manufacturers made models of either cars: only a cardboard cut-out from Kellogg's Sugar Smacks and a jigsaw puzzle – both of Bessie – remain as much sought-after souvenirs among fans.)

Jon was able to indulge his passion for speed *and* combine his nostalgia for the sea when filming *The Sea Devils* by Malcolm Hulke in 1971 on locations around Portsmouth in Hampshire. The story, with its Citroën Deux Chevaux car chase, motorboats sailing at high speed on the sea and a breathtaking climb up a deserted sea fort on the Solent, enabled Jon (who liked to do all the stunts himself) to turn the show into 'a kind of science fiction James Bond', as he later described it. There were a number of amusing moments during the filming, especially around Whale Island which brought back memories for Jon of his *Navy Lark* days.

The Sea Devils themselves reminded the star of something quite different. With their pursed mouths and staring eyes he thought they looked exactly like his cavalier spaniel, Digby! Jon always thought it rather bizarre that the devils wore what looked like blue coloured string vests which were actually supposed to be the remains of fishermen's nets they had picked up from the bottom of the ocean.

Another moment from this location shoot – which received the blessing of the Navy and entailed the cast and film crew spending six days of shooting on HMS *Frazer* – became one of his favourite stories for retelling to fans.

'We were filming this scene on the beach at Portsmouth where six Sea Devils were supposed to emerge from the water,' he said. 'Now the heads of the Sea Devils actually sat on top of the actors' own heads and as soon as they tried to submerge themselves for the take, the air inside made the heads pop straight up to the surface. In the end, the heads had to be filled with water after which the poor chaps came spluttering up the beach, almost drowning. It's a good job their language wasn't on the sound track!'

Probably Jon's most fearsome enemy was the Master, an arch-villain the equal, some said, of Sherlock Holmes's enemy Moriarty or James Bond's Blofeld. Created by Robert Holmes for *Terror of the Autons* (January 1971), he is a Time Lord like the Doctor, though more of a renegade pursuing his own evil ends. Played with mesmerising panache by Roger Delgado, both the character and the actor quickly became revered in *Doctor Who* circles. Since Delgado's tragic death in 1973, the role has been regenerated twice by Anthony Ainley and Eric Roberts, and briefly played by Geoffrey Beevers and Peter Pratt.

As his companions in danger, Jon had Jo Grant played by Katy Manning (who after leaving the show notoriously posed nude with a Dalek), the beautiful science graduate Liz Shaw (played by Caroline John, 1970), and the attractive reporter Sarah Jane Smith (Elisabeth Sladen, 1973–6) who shared the Doctor's exploits in the Whomobile and later continued as Tom Baker's assistant when Jon left the show. There was also the trio of UNIT officers, Brigadier Alastair Lethbridge-Stewart (Nicholas Courtney, 1968–), the regular soldier, Sergeant John Benton (John Levene, 1968–75) and the dashing young Captain Mike Yates (Richard Franklin, 1971–4).

One element of the series that Jon Pertwee loathed were the Daleks. 'I just think they are boring,' he said candidly, 'but people seem to love them so I suppose I am wrong. I'm not a great lover of science fiction, but I am inclined to believe in UFOs. But why won't the blighters land?'

He was always very quick to defend the show against claims of being horrific – a factor which was to become much more contentious during the time of his successor.

The Doctor's companion Jo Grant (Katy Manning) became so attached to the Daleks that she posed in the nude with one after leaving the series!

The Doctor's arch-rival, the Master, originally played by Roger Delgado.

'It's got to be a bit scary,' he said on one occasion. 'My boy has a place under the table where he watches it from. But he doesn't have nightmares about it. He *likes* being scared by it. If parents write to me and say their kids are scared, I write back and say: "Well, it's very simple. You lean forward, put out your hand, and turn the switch to the off position."'

Jon did enjoy being reunited with Patrick Troughton and William Hartnell to make *The Three Doctors*, though because the first Doctor was so ill they only spent one day together filming at Elstree and another at Bill's cottage where they all posed for publicity photographs.

'Although Bill was obviously very poorly, he did well reading his lines from cue cards,' Jon recalled. 'It was a special moment being with this man who had started the whole ball rolling, and with Pat, too, who had lost none of his old sense of humour. I think we gave Bill a laugh or two that day in Elstree, but he must have been under a terrible strain.'

After five years, Jon himself was also beginning to show the strain of playing the Doctor.

'When you play the Doctor you have most of the responsibility for the success of the series on your shoulders,' he said frankly. 'That can put a lot of pressure on you as both Bill and Pat found. I always did my best to make everyone feel as if they were part of a team and we did laugh a lot and even behaved very badly at times. But I know I have a temper which I can't always control and there were times when I threw my weight about and made demands. I do tend to speak my mind and I can be intolerant. It was sometimes very hard not to be impatient with other people when working against a tight schedule, and I know the strain got to me at times. There were certainly times on *Doctor Who* when I was *very* impatient. I like to think now, though, that those people understood. I hope so.'

During my meetings with Jon, he was always delightful company, a constant source of anecdotes which were often hilarious, sometimes apocryphal, and occasionally so scandalous they could never be repeated. All of them told in that mixture of voices which had earned him the epithet, 'The Man of a Thousand Voices'. In public, though, he preferred to appear as the Doctor.

'Throughout the time I played the character I always turned up in public in the frilly shirt and cloak,' he said in words that echoed almost exactly those of his friend Pat Troughton. 'People love the character, not

Jon Pertwee. I can't bear going to parties as myself and I hate entering rooms full of people. I think people think I'm an arrogant bastard when I walk in, but my demeanour is hiding my shyness.'

Jon Pertwee bowed out of *Doctor Who* in *Planet of the Spiders* by Robert Sloman in June 1974. It proved a most suitable culmination to his years as the Doctor, allowing him to take the wheel of Bessie and the Whomobile, race a speedboat, drive a hovercraft and fly an autogyro – although he was not actually allowed to take off from the ground.

Within eighteen months of leaving the series, Jon had achieved what can prove so difficult for many actors: reinventing himself in a completely new character, the scruffy, talking scarecrow, *Worzel Gummidge*; a series by Keith Waterhouse and Willis Hall which ran for four years, although it never had quite the same sort of mass appeal as *Doctor Who*.

In 1974, Jon was to have appeared in a London stage play, *Doctor Who and the Daleks in Seven Keys to Doomsday* specially written for him by Terrance Dicks, but was prevented from doing so by other commitments, and so the role was taken instead by Trevor Martin. (See *Who Is the Doctor on Stage.*) He did, though, appear in another play, *Doctor Who – The Ultimate Adventure*, also written by Terrance Dicks, in 1986. (This production was to have a second run in 1989 with Colin Baker in the lead role.) Jon also reappeared in the anniversary special, *The Five Doctors* and in several radio adaptations – including *Doctor Who and the Paradise of Death* (to mark the show's thirtieth anniversary in November 1993) and *Doctor Who: The Ghosts of N Space* (in January 1996), both written by Barry Letts and co-starring Elisabeth Sladen and Nicholas Courtney. He also spent several years in his own one-man show, *Who is Jon Pertwee?* which drew heavily on his experiences as the Doctor.

Jon retained a number of souvenirs from the series which he was always happy to show off. In the back garden of his Barnes home he kept a statue of Bok the gargoyle from *The Daemons* by Guy Leopold (1971) and he shipped several of his 'toys' out to his holiday home in Ibiza including the water-scooters used in *The Sea Devils* and the Hamilton jet-boat in which he had skimmed across the waves in *Planet of the Spiders*.

Tragically, like his predecessor, Jon Pertwee died of a heart attack, while he was on holiday in America on 20 May 1996. If he had any regrets that his career had not made him the kind of international star his incredible versatility might have deserved, Jon's importance to the legend of *Doctor Who* can never be underestimated.

Who Is the Doctor on Stage

Trevor Martin, the actor who took the role intended for Jon Pertwee in *Doctor Who and the Daleks in Seven Keys to Doomsday* in 1974, was, in fact, already acquainted with the mystique of the Doctor, having appeared as a Time Lord in Patrick Troughton's final appearance in *The War Games* (1969). But although the part in the production at the Adelphi Theatre in London earned Trevor similar nationwide publicity to his predecessors, because he appeared 'between Doctors' he is not considered as part of the Time Lord's 'genealogy'.

Trevor Martin, who appeared as the Doctor on stage in 1974.

The play, by Terrance Dicks, provided the Doctor with two companions: Wendy Padbury, who had formerly been Zoe Herriott, playing Jenny, and James Matthews as Jimmy. The story involved the trio in a race to prevent the Daleks from seizing the Crystal of All Power – currently in seven pieces on the planet Karn – which would arm them with the Ultimate Weapon and enable them to conquer the galaxy. As a matter of interest, certain elements of the play with its giant, lobster-like, Clawrentulars and showpiece psychic battle between the Doctor and the Master of Karn (played by Simon Jones who was later to become famous as Arthur Dent in *The Hitch-Hiker's Guide to the Galaxy*) were adapted by Terrance Dicks in 1976 for his Tom Baker story, *The Brain of Morbius*.

Trevor Martin, a tall, classically trained actor who had worked for the Prospect Theatre Company and just prior to the play become well known to millions of TV viewers as Arthur Whittaker in *Coronation Street*, was given the role after several actors were auditioned by the director, Mick Hughes. Trevor believes he got the role because he was in the same middle-aged bracket as the other Doctors and was also an experienced stage actor. He said of the part in a subsequent interview:

'I felt it was time for a change from classical roles. My approach to the part was only influenced a little bit by what had been seen on television. I tried to keep my own interpretation and concentrated on being *real*. I knew that basically all the situations, the creatures I met with and the mechanical gadgets that were used did not exist. So I started out from the premise that if such things *did* exist, my reactions to them must be as real as possible.'

Trevor decided on making his Doctor look a little bit like all his predecessors on television, with a long white wig (Hartnell), baggy check trousers (Troughton) and a stylish plum-coloured coat (Pertwee). And because the Time Lord had last been seen on television in the process of regenerating, the play's designer, John Napier, opened with a giant screen showing Pertwee's face changing into that of Trevor Martin.

'Your face! It's different,' the opening line of dialogue spoken by young James ran. 'Oh, no,' the Doctor replied, 'not again!'

The production had reached the West End through the perseverance of two new producers – both fans of the series – Anthony Pye-Jeary and Robert De Winter who had spent the previous ten months raising the £35,000 needed to stage the show with its lavish sets, five Daleks, enormous 'Doomsday Machine' and 24 carousel slide projectors all linked together to provide the special effects.

Seven Keys to Doomsday played to packed houses after its opening on 16 December and was well reviewed. 'The production is absolutely splendid and concentrates on accuracy to the original sources,' wrote B.A. Young of the *Guardian*. 'The Daleks are a living legend now – even more widely known than the Hobbits.'

After its planned four-week run at the Adelphi, it was intended that the production would go on a nationwide tour, culminating in a summer season at Blackpool. But, tragically, the IRA instigated another of its terror campaigns that Christmas, setting off bomb scares throughout the West End which seriously disrupted the capital and kept audiences away from the show.

'It was a sad ending,' Trevor Martin said later, 'and perhaps if it had succeeded I might have even got to play the Doctor on television. Who knows?'

A rare copy of the poster which advertised *Seven Keys to Doomsday* in 1974.

A Traveller of Many Worlds

The day was hot and sunny and along the King's Road in Chelsea men in multicoloured t-shirts and women in frocks and jeans were mingling with tourists of all nationalities. Ever since the early sixties when the first boutiques opened selling mini-skirts and psychedelic trousers, this particular street has been a mecca for people anxious to see and be seen, and only those conventionally dressed ever look out of place. With Sloane Square, the habit of the famous Sloane Rangers at one end, and a pub aptly named the World's End at the other, the impression is very strong that King's Road might just be one of the most interesting places on earth.

So where better to meet Tom Baker, the Doctor who travelled to more alien worlds and more cities on the face of the Earth and did most to turn *Doctor Who* into a world-wide cult than anyone else? In fact, Tom lived for several years in this world of fashionably baroque clothes stores and food shops, antique arcades, restaurants and pubs, and memories of him linger on in the minds of those people who knew him and still live in what is an area unique for its history and pageantry. It was here, too, that his particular odyssey as the Doctor began.

I have met Tom on several occasions. Once in the garden of Henry J. Bean's, on the King's Road, a fashionable bar which had been a pub frequented by Charles II. I also shared a long and alcoholic lunch in Soho with him and some friends; and our paths crossed again a few years ago when he was working on the hospital drama series *Medics* in Manchester. But of all these places, while Tom was playing the Doctor he was happiest around the King's Road. 'I used to live upstairs there,' he told me as we

TOM BAKER

ACTOR: Tom Baker (1934–)

TIME-SPAN: 1974–81

CHARACTERISTICS: **Unpredictable, witty and perhaps the most alien of all the Time Lords. Capable of defeating his enemies with moments of unlikely inspiration, he was very much the larger-than-life Doctor who needed both his hearts to sustain his almost manic bursts of energy.**

APPEARANCE: **Bohemian in style, the Doctor's clothes varied considerably during his seven years in space and time – though his trademarks were undoubtedly his broad-brimmed, floppy hat and seventeen-foot long multicoloured scarf. His first red coat had patched elbows and this was subsequently replaced by versions in dark brown and tweed. Most of his pairs of trousers were also tweed. He had a variety of waistcoats and patterned cardigans. In his final year, the Doctor had a matching costume all in burgundy.**

sat in the sweltering heat of the garden at Henry J. Bean's, indicating the seventeenth-century building behind us. 'The best part of the district. It's less Breughel here.'

Tom is one of life's unforgettable characters. The wild blue eyes, the mouth full of huge teeth, and his rangy, 6 ft 3 ins frame make him an impressive figure even before he speaks. And when he does talk, the words spill out almost too fast to catch and are so enthralling that to sit and listen is the best thing. Tom is a true entertainer whether he has a script or not, and the anecdotes which flow from him are a mixture of the apocryphal and the remarkable – and it is often difficult to tell which is which. His period as the Doctor remains among his fondest memories and the stories he told me about his work then – and has recounted in the years since – make his one of the most remarkable eras in the show's history. To some he is the man who made the series; the best of all the Doctors. What is certain is that his impact on the legend was paramount and will never be forgotten.

Tom Baker at an impromptu press call on the beach at Brighton while filming *The Leisure Hive* in 1980.

As we sat discussing *Doctor Who* – and I tried, often in vain, to prevent him veering off the subject as is his inclination in any conversation – a group of builders were working just beyond the pub's garden wall. When Tom finally caught sight of them, he paused for a moment. 'Seeing those chaps brings it all back,' he said pointing in their direction. 'Because I was working on a building site, broke, and with no prospect of work when I was offered the part of the Doctor. It was just the most extraordinary thing . . .'

Tom sat back in his seat and took another drink. I had already done my research into his life and knew something of his background, so with this remark the whole story of the Doctor who took on the worlds of Earth, space and time began to fit into place.

Tom Baker was born on 20 January 1934 in Fountains Road, Liverpool; the tough Scotland Road area of the city. The only son of Thomas and Mary Jane Baker, he remembers a childhood haunted by poverty and religion with his father, a Merchant Navy seaman, often away, and his mother working all hours as a cleaner and barmaid.

'I was brought up among Irish pubs and Irish priests,' he says, 'and brainwashed with this preoccupation with death. Which is perhaps why I still like to wander around graveyards collecting strange epitaphs. From the age of five I was constantly at confession until I dried up of sins to confess.'

He remembers an even more grisly occasion as a child standing with his father in St George's Hall, Liverpool, listening to the words, 'Kelly's going to swing'. It was during the trial of George Kelly who was later hanged for the murder of a local cinema manager, and the words still slip back into his mind at moments of anxiety. On the lighter side, Tom enjoyed helping out his aunt who was a street bookmaker – an unlawful activity then – and remembers that many punters put strange names on their illegal betting slips. Valentine Dyall – the actor and radio broadcaster famous for his series *The Man in Black* (1941–53) – was a popular choice apparently, and it is a source of amusement to Tom that he later actually appeared with the sepulchral-voiced veteran in *Doctor Who*. (Valentine Dyall was also twice listed as a possible Doctor *himself*, but ultimately made four appearances in the late seventies and early eighties as the personification of evil, the Black Guardian.)

Tom's early heroes were characters in the comics *Adventure, Wizard* and *Hotspur* which enabled him to escape the real-life horrors of the Second World War with German bombs dropping all over Liverpool. As time passed, his desire to leave the grind of city life grew ever stronger, and when a priest visited the Richard Kelly Catholic School where he was a pupil and suggested that because of his religious upbringing he might like to consider the priesthood, he didn't hesitate. So, at the age of fifteen Tom entered the Order of Ploermel on the island of Jersey and later moved to another monastery in Shropshire for his noviciate.

'For five years I dug the gardens and stoked the boilers and got up at 5.15 a.m. to say *Veni Spiritus Sancti* with the brothers,' he has recalled. 'It all brought me to the edge of a nervous breakdown and made me realise I would never make a priest. So I renounced my vows, went home, and almost straight away was called up to do two years' National Service in the Royal Army Medical Corps.'

It was while he was in the Army that Tom began to realise he could act. He had always been able to use his sense of humour to talk himself out of difficult situations with bigger and older boys. Then during his service in the RAMC, he was 'coerced' into appearing in a unit show and once he had overcome his nervousness and climbed on stage found he had a natural ability to make people laugh. This gift has now seen him through both the good and bad days of his career.

After completing his National Service, Tom followed in his father's footsteps by joining the Merchant Navy and for several years sailed between Britain and the USA on ships like the *Queen Mary*. But growing tired of this, he decided to pursue his inclination for acting by joining a drama school, and got a place at the Rose Bruford College of Speech and Drama in Sidcup, Kent where he trained for three years. Work was not easy to come by for a raw young actor in the late fifties, and after appearing on the repertory circuit in productions like *Hindle Wakes* and *Stop it, Nurse*, he and a friend from student days, Laurie Taylor, put together a fringe comedy show at the York Festival, *Late Night Lowther*, in which the most outstanding sketch had Tom playing a talking dog, Clint, with Laurie Taylor as his brutal trainer.

Tom still chuckles at this, one of the defining moments in his life. 'I was seen playing the dog by someone from the National Theatre and invited to go to the Old Vic. Laurence Olivier auditioned me and he must have seen something because he offered me a part in *The Trials of Sancho Panza* – as a horse! Things looked up after that and I got to play human beings. It was a very happy time for me and Olivier encouraged me a lot and helped me to get the part of Rasputin in *Nicholas and Alexandra*.'

The Sam Spiegel film made in 1971 provided Tom with an ideal opportunity to bring the full range of his mannerisms to the role of the mad Russian monk – to which he added some of the agonies and ecstasies he had experienced himself in Jersey and Shropshire. The film was a critical and commercial success and kept Tom busy into the seventies with parts in the theatre and movies, including *The Golden Voyage of Sinbad* in which he played an evil magician, Prince Loura. (He was also, he says, considered for playing the creature in Christopher Isherwood's *Frankenstein: The True Story* but the producer decided he wanted an actor who was 'more of a name and a lot more handsome!')

In 1973, Tom found himself out of work once again and, never too proud to take any job when he was hard up, got a job as a builder's labourer in Ebury Street, London. He soon became popular with the other workmen because of his endless fund of stories, although, as he says, they called him 'Sir Laurence' and often 'took the piss'. Unbeknownst to him as he alternately mixed concrete or worked a Kango drill, a BBC director named Bill Slater, for whom he had played a doctor in the BBC2 production of *The Millionairess* starring Maggie Smith, was about to change his whole life. Bill was then the head of the department in which

The Doctor comforts his injured companion, Sarah Jane Smith (Elisabeth Sladen), during filming of *The Hand of Fear* (1976).

The anatomy of a Dalek revealing the major components including the scanner, combat computer, environment chamber in which the 'living' Dalek is housed, vocal simulator, multi-range power destructor, hostility sensors, auto-destruct and motor unit to enable it to move.

Barry Letts, now the producer of *Doctor Who*, worked; and, aware that Jon Pertwee was leaving the series, suggested Tom as his replacement. Among the other actors being considered at the time were Richard Hearn, Graham Crowden, Jim Dale, Fulton McKay and even the ex-Goon Michael Bentine; but after watching Tom's performance in *The Golden Voyage of Sinbad* the production team opted for him. On 16 February 1973 he went, overnight, from labourer to Time Lord.

'On the day the news was announced I went to the building site as usual,' Tom told me as we sat in the King's Road pub still watching the workmen nearby. 'They just couldn't believe it. But they were all so kind and when a photographer came along to take a picture for the *Daily Express* I insisted that they were all in it. I was *almost* sorry to leave them.'

The euphoria of landing the role did not leave Tom for some days and it was not until a reporter asked him if he planned to play the Doctor with a Liverpool accent that he realised he would have to give some thought to the character he wanted to present. Unlike his predecessors, he had never watched *Doctor Who* so he had no preconceived notions. Because of comments in the press that his manic grin and unruly long brown hair gave him a resemblance to Harpo Marx, the BBC suggested that wearing a white wig or a deerstalker hat might be suitable. Tom, though, felt the answer probably lay in a combination of his natural energy, personality and eccentricity, and came up with the idea of looking like a bohemian artist of the type so familiar in Paris in the twenties and – just occasionally – in the King's Road of the day. He could have no inkling he would soon become one of the most instantly recognised and most widely imitated of all the Doctors!

In a sentence, Tom Baker created the new Doctor out of *himself*. 'I am always being asked about the methods I use and the thoughts that go through my mind when I am acting,' he says, 'but the honest answer is I don't know. When I first started on *Doctor Who* I just tried to anticipate how the Doctor would react to the situations in which he found himself as he went along. I suppose it was a happy accident when we found that it was working!'

The first story Tom filmed as the Doctor in April 1974, *Robot* by Terrance Dicks, contained a regeneration scene with Jon Pertwee, a first meeting with Elisabeth Sladen as his companion who he says was wonderful to him (and remains his favourite assistant), and then a running battle with a huge metal monster played by an actor even taller than

(Left) The TARDIS console as seen at the *Doctor Who* exhibition in Blackpool.

(Below) A scene from *The Daleks: Invasion Earth 2150 AD* with Bernard Cribbins, Peter Cushing and Jill Curzon.

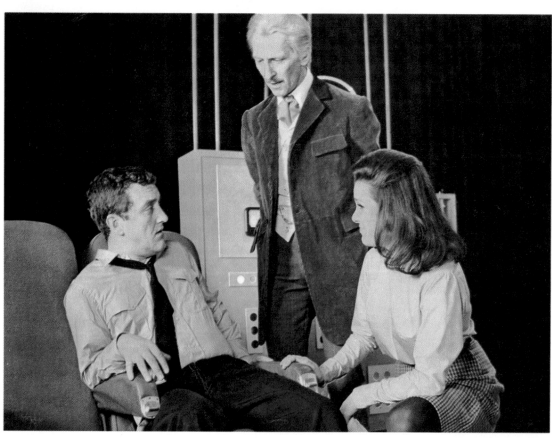

(Above) Filming *The Abominable Snowmen* in Wales in September 1967.

(Left) Not Godzilla, but a dinosaur on the rampage in Derbyshire in *Doctor Who and the Silurians* (1970).

(Above) A not uncommon spot of bother with Bessie for Jon Pertwee and his companion Liz Shaw (Caroline John).

(Right) Tom Baker met Lalla Ward when she played his companion, Romana II, in *The Armageddon Factor* in 1978. Later, they were briefly married.

(Above) The amazing world of pleasure for galactic travellers on the planet Argolis from *The Leisure Hive* (1980) designed by Tom Yardley-Jones.

(Right) The Doctor's arch-enemy and fellow Time Lord, the Master, in his second regeneration played by Anthony Ainley.

Two of the rarest *Doctor Who* collectables – a Patrick Troughton annual and a battery-operated Dalek, both from the 1960s.

(Above) A line-up of Doctors including Tom Baker's dummy and Richard Hurndall (far right), who replaced William Hartnell at the press call to promote *The Five Doctors* in 1983.

(Left) Colin Baker and his companion Melanie Bush (Bonnie Langford) share a joke at the studios in 1986.

(Above) Sylvester McCoy on location in Wales in the summer of 1987 for *Delta and the Bannermen* with Ken Dodd and Don Henderson.

(Right) Looking into the future: Paul McGann, like everyone else, has cause to wonder just *what* might happen to the Doctor next ...

himself, Michael Kilgarrif. Tom, who had of course played every kind of role including a dog, struck up an instant rapport with Kilgarrif who was actually a well-known music hall artist renowned for his Edwardian monologues. Tom was amused to learn that Kilgarrif, who is 6 ft 7 ins tall, had achieved something of a monopoly playing huge monsters in the series. *Robot*, however, was to prove very different from the rest.

'My costume was incredibly heavy and claustrophobic and I could hardly move in it,' Michael Kilgarrif recalled later. 'When we were on location at Wood Norton I kept toppling over or falling to my knees. The whole experience gave me horrific nightmares about getting trapped in the suit. So I told the director Christopher Barry that I couldn't go on wearing it through all the rehearsals. So they provided me with a lightweight version which consisted of just the head and shoulders and the feet and claws. I only put the full outfit on at the last moment when we were filming – but I still don't know how I got through it.'

Michael Kilgarrif played the huge robot in Tom Baker's first story, *Robot*, filmed in 1974.

Tom Baker on location
with his stand-in and
stunt man, Terry
Walsh.

Tom soon got into his stride as the Doctor and just as quickly began making his own input into the series; not to mention using his energy and eccentricity to galvanise those producing the series – and those watching it. While the vast majority of the viewers found him every bit as good as his predecessors, there was the odd dissenting voice such as 12-year-old Nicholas Franklin who wrote to the *Sun*.

'The new Doctor is too weak,' Nicholas said. 'He doesn't fight the robots and monsters. He runs away or tries to trick them. I can't believe in him because he looks and acts like a student. He's too jokey. He doesn't seem to take his adventures seriously. When I watch a programme on telly I want to believe it's happening – but I can't with this man. He seems to think he's in a pantomime. Five of my school friends agree with me.'

Making *The Sontaran Experiment* by Bob Baker and Dave Martin proved anything but a joke for Tom Baker. While filming a fight scene on Dartmoor in September, he slipped and fell and broke his collar bone. The result was that he couldn't move without pain and had to be taken to hospital.

'It was all wonderfully dramatic as I was being carried across the moors on a stretcher,' he said later. 'But I was a bit deflated when I got to hospital and was told that broken collar bones were everyday occurrences whenever rugby was being played. I still managed to have a laugh when I got back to the hotel and found some of the others sitting solemnly in the bar obviously thinking they had lost their leading actor. And there I suddenly was offering to buy them all a drink!'

In fact, for the next three days the series' regular stunt man Terry Walsh, who was also Tom's stand-in, doubled for him in all the scenes that required action by the Doctor, while Baker was filmed in close up with his arm strapped in a sling out of sight of the camera. It was a lesson to him, he said, about overdoing fight scenes and he was never going to be quite so heroic again. It was also the start of his friendship with Terry Walsh who had been with the series since the days of William Hartnell and would continue for the next decade to bring his expertise at being blown up, run over, falling off cliffs, driving all kinds of motor vehicles, fighting with virtually any weapon, and being stand-in for the incumbent Time Lord.

A new producer, Philip Hinchcliffe, supervised Tom's introduction to the Doctor's oldest enemies in *Genesis of the Daleks* by Terry Nation and *Revenge of the Cybermen* by Gerry Davis. Tom has always accepted the popularity of the Daleks, but was never able to take them totally seriously after the first day of rehearsals when he saw the operators going through their scenes with the tops of the machines removed, holding out their right arms to simulate the guns!

Genesis of the Daleks also saw the introduction of the crippled genetic scientist, Davros, who had invented the Daleks. Played by Michael Wisher in a special face mask sitting in his life support machine, the character proved unforgettable to viewers . . . and Tom.

'It was painfully funny during rehearsals with Mike Wisher,' Tom recalls, 'because he used to wear this paper bag over his head to get into character. Watching him just reduced me to tears on several occasions.'

There was also a funny side to *Revenge of the Cybermen*. Tom suggested to script editor Robert Holmes that the story might contain a scene where he and Elisabeth Sladen were captured, tied to a post, and made to look on while the Cybermen were studying a film clip of Fred Astaire and Ginger Rogers dancing in order to copy the

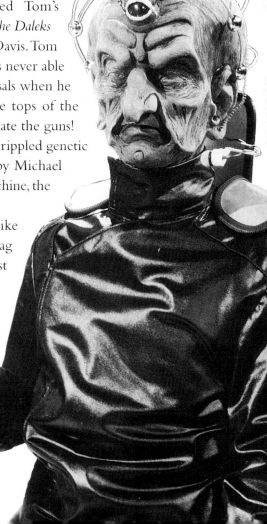

Davros, the Dalek mastermind played several times by Michael Wisher, could never quite remove the smile from the Doctor's face!

way they moved. Holmes, perhaps understandably, rejected the idea – but retained the captivity scene. A line in the story brought the studios to a standstill while the couple were roped together and facing one another and the Doctor said they were 'facing the biggest bang in history'!

In April 1975 Tom got first-hand experience of what it was like to play a monster in the story, *Pyramids of Mars* by Stephen Harris. In order to stop the evil Sutekh and his force of robots dressed as mummies, the Doctor was required to disguise himself in one of the costumes. The scenes were filmed at Newbury in Berkshire – actually in the grounds of Stargroves, a house that belonged to Mick Jagger – and because the director, Paddy Russell, decided Tom's walk was inimitable, he insisted that he put on one of the mummy costumes which were made of thick bandages over a wire shell with the leggings held up by braces. He remembers playing the scene was terribly difficult and he nearly suffocated inside the costume!

With the viewing audience for *Doctor Who* in excess of twelve million by 1976, it was clear that Tom Baker had made the Doctor very much his own, as Nancy Mills wrote in a full-page article in the *Guardian*.

'The BBC took an enormous gamble casting such a quick-witted, aggressive personality as Baker in a father figure role,' she wrote. 'But he was an inspired choice. He has turned the character into a cult figure, replete with fans clubs and *Doctor Who* societies all over Britain. It is rumoured that a university administrator recently broke up a student demonstration by announcing that *Doctor Who* was on the television. By the time they realised it was only Tuesday, it was too late.'

For his part, Tom knew that fame had taken over his life. 'I have to keep reminding myself that I do not have an existence as Tom Baker,' he told Peter Dacre of the *Sunday Express*. 'With a TV programme like *Doctor Who* which had entered the national consciousness, you become a part of everybody's life. Everyone, even children in the street, look at me as the Doctor. They are not looking at *me*, though, but as this image they have of the character. I therefore have to be sure not to disappoint people, especially the children. It is important to me never to be seen being raucous in the streets, or plastered, or smoking cigars.'

In fact – as Tom is now prepared to admit – his days as the Doctor were 'mad times' whenever he was away from the cameras seeking a little diversion. Indeed, he became a familiar sight in Soho on many nights with a hard-drinking crowd of friends including the painter Francis Bacon

and the journalist Jeffrey Bernard. 'It was a marvellous haze induced by the most popular drug in the world,' he reflects. 'And being with people who did miraculous things – Jeffrey with his wonderful column in the *Spectator* and Francis with his amazing paintings – I don't know what they were about – and his prodigious capacity to make us all laugh, and his fabulous wealth which he poured on us all. Of course, there were casualties. People fell down stairs or their livers exploded, but the tragedies just made us madder and madder.'

Although Tom undoubtedly relished this lifestyle for a while, he did stick to his vow – especially where children were concerned. I remember walking along Old Compton Street with him and several others after a lunch at which vast quantities of vodka and white wine had been consumed (by some of the party in a shattering mixture of both!) to be suddenly confronted by a small boy and his parents, all of whom instantly recognised him. With astonishing dexterity, Tom discarded the cigar between his fingers quicker than the eye could see, strangled the laugh in his throat, and fixed

Tom Baker found out what it was like to be one of the monsters he usually confronted when playing a robot mummy in *Pyramids of Mars* (1975).

his famous goggle-eyed smile on the child. 'Hello,' he said to the little boy, 'haven't I seen you before? Yes, I know, I've seen you watching television!' It was obviously a well-rehearsed line, but none the less effective for that, and the child's giggle of delight was instantaneous. Reaching into the bag slung over his shoulder, Tom extracted one of the personal photographs he always carried, asked the boy his name, and quickly wrote on it, 'To David. Who on Earth is Tom Baker?' and then strode off into the night with all of us still enjoying his performance in his wake.

I remember that he also told me on that occasion that *Doctor Who* was not an acting part, but a matter of being inventive enough to project credibility on scenes that weren't credible. He described it as a hovercraft that was on a fine line all the same, never quite daring to touch the ground.

In *The Face of Evil* by Chris Boucher the Doctor was joined by a new companion: the exotic, leather-clad Sevateem warrior, Leela, played by Louise James (1977–8), and replacing Elisabeth Sladen. Tom has said that he was never very keen on this character because of her propensity to violence (though this was toned down by Louise) and did not like it when the series was attacked by Mary Whitehouse and a number of newspaper critics in 1978. The reasons given were that it had a 'harmful effect' on children, giving some of them nightmares and causing others to wet the bed. Tom and Robert Holmes in a series of interviews resolutely defended *Doctor Who* from this criticism, saying that it was essential for the Doctor to be 'a man of courage and morality'.

Nor did he find it any easier to work with K9, the dog-like mobile computer which first appeared in *The Invisible Enemy* by Bob Baker and Dave Martin and thereafter became a part of the Doctor's entourage as well as a great favourite with fans. Tom did, though, enjoy the rehearsals at which John Leeson, the actor who provided the voice for K9, would impersonate a dog with the same kind of enthusiasm and wit that he himself had once brought to a similar role. When the actual robot went wrong during filming, however, he was quite likely to kick it in frustration. His final verdict on the dog which remained with him for four years, inspired a sequel, *K9 and Company*, and is about to return to television in a new series, was 'insufferable'. (See *K9: The Doctor's Robot Dog*.)

Promoting the series was, though, never hard work for Tom and he enjoyed trips to America and Australia where *Doctor Who* was a big hit. He especially liked doing charity work involving children and the *Sun* ran a special feature on this element of his life after he had spent several days visiting hospitals in Blackpool, Blackburn, Liverpool and Preston cheering up sick and injured children. He told the paper's reporter, Liz Prosser:

'It was no good being over-jolly or letting it upset me. I had to keep my tears hidden deep inside. I saw a kid who'd been run over. His limbs were gnarled, his eyes out of focus as if he'd had a stroke. His mother was trying vainly to get his mind back – it was appalling. There was also a boy with smashed legs who'd become pally with the woman motorist whose car had hit him.

'I saw dozens of kids, most of them terribly maimed in road accidents, often by drunken drivers. Also children dumped by cruel or inadequate parents. How can these children victims happen when there are so many men and women with love locked away in their hearts who yearn for children of their own, can't have them and can't adopt? *Doctor Who* has brought me so much, the least I can do is make this romantic hero useful where it really matters – with the less-fortunate kids.'

Tom also found that as a result of meeting children generally he was able to keep the role fresh. Unlike adults, he said, small boys and girls were very direct in their opinions and he often incorporated pieces of advice they had given him into later stories. His extraordinary rapport with youngsters is something in which he still delights, and he puts this down to his ability not to make them feel threatened. He says they probably like him because they feel superior!

'Do you know something,' he told me on one occasion, 'for five years children ran towards me when they recognised me without having to be warned by their parents about talking to a strange man. *That* was an amazing pleasure.'

The other side of the coin were the older, female fans who had sexual designs on him when he was on personal appearance tours. In Boston for one convention he was greeted by a well-endowed brunette who said directly, 'My name's Melissa and I'm from Concorde and I'm in love with you.' Tom remembers such occasions with a broad grin: 'There were a lot of dotty people who wanted to shag the Doctor. And sometimes, of course, I gave in. I'll certainly never forget one girl who said, "Come on Doctor, let's travel through space".'

The fifteenth season of the series saw the arrival of yet another new producer, Graham Williams, with whom Tom says he always had a slightly awkward relationship; a new companion, the Time Lord, Lady Romana played by Mary Tamm (1978–9) in *The Ribos Operation* by Robert

Holmes; and shortly afterwards a new script editor, Douglas Adams, already working on the radio series which would ultimately turn him into a celebrated best-selling author, *The Hitch-Hiker's Guide to the Galaxy*. Despite the renewal of energy provided by this trio, Tom admits he was now feeling as proprietorial about the role as William Hartnell had done fifteen years earlier and inclined to get angry when scenes did not go well or the way he thought they should. He also believes that his performance as the Doctor was becoming more operatic and sensed there was a danger of the series becoming a parody of itself.

Filming the series on location was never easy for the cast and crew and this was especially true when *The Power of Kroll* by Robert Holmes was shot in August 1978 at Iken in Suffolk not far from where I live. This is a rather remote little community with a population of eighty on the banks of the River Alde with picturesque marshlands all around. The promontory at Iken – with the church of St Botolph's, one of the earliest Christian sites in the country – was used as the set of Delta Magna's third moon. Here a feud is in progress between the original humanoid inhabitants, the Swampies, and some human technicians, into which the Doctor and Romana are plunged.

Filming a scene in 1979 for the Douglas Adams story, *Shada*, which was never completed or broadcast because of a strike at the BBC.

Tom remembers that the film crew had to keep moving because of the rising tides of the Alde and also to make sure there was nothing out of character on the horizon. The Swampies had to be sprayed green each morning before filming began and then scrubbed raw in the evening to remove the paint. He himself tripped over his famous scarf and fell into some water which caused a delay while he had to make a complete change of costume.

The next story, *The Armageddon Factor* by Bob Baker and Dave Martin, introduced yet another companion, the second incarnation of Romana, played by Lalla Ward (1979–81) whom the Doctor rescued from the clutches of the Black Guardian (Valentine Dyall). Tom did more than rescue Lalla: off-screen he courted her, the petite, blonde Honourable Sarah Ward, daughter of Viscount Bangor; and in November 1980 announced that despite all his protestations in the past that he wanted to remain a bachelor, the couple were to marry. It was, in fact, Tom's second marriage; his first to Anna Wheatcroft, daughter of the famous rose-grower, Harry Wheatcroft, by whom he had two sons, Daniel and Piers (now in their thirties), ended in divorce in 1966.

'I felt something very right from day one – the day Lalla started to work on the show two years ago,' Tom told the press. 'It was only when Lalla finished, leaving me to carry on with my last series alone, that we both realised we had to make the fateful decision to get married.'

The marriage, at Chelsea Register Office on 13 December 1980 lasted for just sixteen months, the reason cited for its failure being conflict of careers. 'I had a marvellous time with Lalla,' he says now. 'It was deliriously short – most marriages last far too long. And we parted in a very friendly way: in fact we parted quite passionately. She has married again very happily to the scientist, Richard Dawkins.'

In May 1979, the whole production team crossed the Channel and went to Paris to film *City of Death* by David Agnew. This was all about a plot to steal the *Mona Lisa* from the Louvre by an alien masquerading as an art collector, Count Scarlioni (Julian Glover), who plans to sell the masterpiece to finance time travel experiments he is conducting. It was the series' first trip abroad and not without incident.

Plans to film a confrontation between the Doctor and the Count at the Coquilles Bar on the Left Bank had to be abandoned when the bar was found to be closed for May Day. By coincidence, the bar next door was called 'Who's – but again the premises were closed. Finally filming was

'… And whosoever knoweth just cause or impediment.' The cartoon by MAC of the *Daily Mail*, 21 November 1980, marking the wedding of Tom Baker and Lalla Ward.

allowed on the terrace of the Café Notre Dame by the patron who, apparently, had never heard of *Doctor Who*. During a chase sequence in the Boulevard St Germain, Tom accidentally set off the burglar alarm at a gallery of modern art when he rattled the door. Although there were crowds around for much of the filming in the city, the enduring memory for the star was being able to walk around the streets without being recognised or stopped because the series was not shown in France.

The man left to make the explanations about the mishaps in Paris was the production unit manager, John Nathan-Turner, who had been working on the series for three years and would shortly afterwards be named as the next producer. But this news was completely overshadowed when Tom announced on 25 October 1980 that he was leaving the series the following March after his final adventure – another deadly battle with The Master (Anthony Ainley) in *Logopolis* by Christopher Bidmead.

Although the BBC had, in fact, already decided on Tom's successor, his sense of mischief got the better of him at his final press conference and he set a hare running that no newspaperman or media correspondent could resist.

'I've enjoyed every single minute of the series,' he said, making no mention of his on-set problems. 'It was never hard work, simply because it was such fun. But I honestly think I've given everything I have to give. I think it's time to let someone else have a go.'

And with a dramatic pause to make sure he had the attention of everyone in the room and a huge grin spreading across his face, he added, 'It could even be a woman. After all, there is no reason why the Doctor should always be a man.'

The feverish speculation which followed resulted in a whole list of names being submitted to the *Doctor Who* office including Jill Gascoine, Maria Aitken, Anna Ford, Pamela Stephenson, Honor Blackman, Jan Leeming and Angela Rippon. Suggestions for a 'mature and a bit eccentric' female Doctor included Beryl Reid, Patricia Hayes, Diana Dors, Annie Walker, politician Shirley Williams and even the Salvation Army's leader, Dame Catharine Bramwell-Booth, then 100 years old and in the words of the *Daily Mail*, 'mature enough to smite all the Doctor's enemies in outer space with the charm of her tongue alone'. Thirteen-year-old Alison Smith of Bristol suggested 'my mummy – because she is daft', while S.J. Moon of Tunbridge Wells wrote that the idea of a female Doctor was ludicrous. 'Time Lords have super powers,' he said, 'but to change their sex is too much to believe!'

Tom's final season in the series – the eighteenth – saw the introduction of the Doctor's first young boy companion, Adric (Matthew Waterhouse, 1980–2), a stowaway from the planet Alzarius in *Full Circle* by Andrew Smith – himself a teenage fan of *Doctor Who*. In the last two episodes, a pair of young girls also joined the team: Nyssa, the striking daughter of Consul Tremas in *The Keeper of Traken* by Johnny Byrne, who was played by Sarah Sutton (1981–3), and the exotic air hostess Tegan Jovanka (Janet Fielding, 1981–3) who became involved in the Doctor's finale in *Logopolis*.

Today, Tom can reflect on his decision to leave the series with the benefit of hindsight and is totally open about the reasons.

'When John [Nathan-Turner] took over it was obvious he wanted to make changes,' he told me. 'He didn't consult me about these changes because it was perfectly obvious that I was already thinking it was time to go. I'd been through four producers and done 178 episodes, and at that point I had become incredibly hard to please because I knew it all. I could be very tactless and overpowering and making demands.

'There were demons working on me long before, telling me to leave and face a new challenge. It had nothing to do with not getting on with John; I just felt I was not getting any better and it was time to go. I thought

I just *can't* be a shagged-out old Doctor Who!'

For a time after leaving *Doctor Who*, Tom deliberately distanced himself from the series. He did not appear in the anniversary special, *The Five Doctors* in 1983 and it was some years before he again agreed to attend conventions. He dramatically changed his appearance – having his trademark locks (now greying) cut short, and wearing a pair of rimless spectacles – although nothing could change the toothy grin. He also married again, to Sue Jerrard, whom he had first met when she was an assistant editor on *Doctor Who*. Today the couple live in a converted Victorian schoolhouse in Kent with their cluster of Burmese cats all named after characters from Dickens, Tom's favourite author.

The roles on the stage and in television which Tom has since appeared in have ranged from Long John Silver, Oscar Wilde and Sherlock Holmes to a quite different type of doctor, the consultant surgeon Professor Geoffrey Hoyt in the Granada series, *Medics*. We met again during the making of this hospital drama in Manchester in 1995 and, inevitably, the topic of *Doctor Who* came up once again. Unlike a number of actors who dislike talking about previous roles with which they have become identified, Tom was quite the reverse.

'*Doctor Who* changed my life,' he said when I taped an interview with him in the series' green room. 'It was the biggest success I ever had and it conferred a kind of immortality on me. I know some people don't like mentioning their past roles and I really don't understand that because we are the products of our past. If you are a public performer you are inextricably linked with what you have appeared in. I was a children's hero for six years and no one will ever be able to take that away from me. There's no end to it if you impersonate *Doctor Who*. You fill the public imagination, and if you fill the public imagination they can't leave you alone.'

Tom has, of course, been able to reap the rewards from his very successful period as the Doctor making public appearances, and recently wrote his autobiography, *Who on Earth is Tom Baker?* (1997) which has become a best-seller. Indeed, he appreciates the commercial value of his association with the series very well. As we parted company on the last occasion, he once again fixed me with that mesmerising look as I was packing away my tape recorder and said, 'Do you know, Peter, that tape would be worth twenty-five dollars a copy on the American *Doctor Who* circuit!'

He roared with laughter as I assured him that I would do no such thing. And I haven't.

K9: The Doctor's Robot Dog

The idea of a robot dog for the Doctor was nurtured into the series' most popular mechanical companion by script editor Robert Holmes, after he had seen the huge success of the two lovable robot heroes, Artoo-Detoo (R2-D2) and See-Threepio (C-3PO), in *Star Wars*. The reference in the script for *The Invisible Enemy* by Bob Baker and Dave Martin to a 'mobile computer that vaguely resembles a dog' was what caught Holmes' eye and made him decide that here was an idea worth developing. What started life with the slightly jokey name 'Fido' was destined to become another landmark in the series.

Once it had been decided to create the robot dog, the task was given to special effects designer, Tony Harding, who captured the concept as it would finally appear with virtually his first rough sketch. The 'working prop', as it was designated, was radio controlled and fitted with a six-channel Futuba set which allowed for ten channels on the AM frequency to cover all of the machine's movements: forwards, backwards, around corners, wagging its tail, moving its antenna, and extending a probe and gun nozzle from its mouth.

A plan of K9's 'anatomy'.

Unfortunately, in the early trials, the camera signals clashed with those meant for K9 and sent the machine haywire. Once this problem was overcome, however, the rear-wheel chain motor engine driving the robot proved to be too noisy on camera and had to be replaced by a front wheel drive with a rubber belt. Thereafter, the dog always had two 'minders' on set to oversee his performance: radio-control specialist, Nigel Brackley, and John Leeson, his 'voice'.

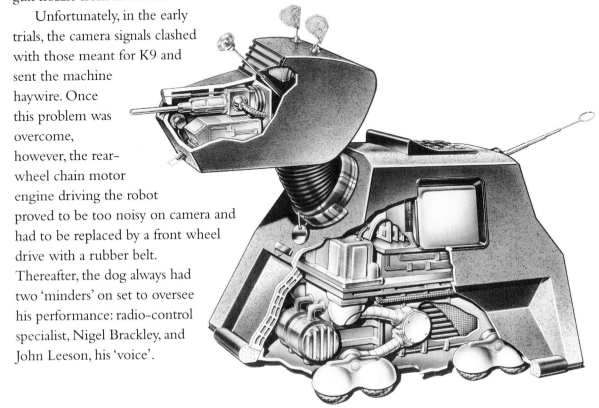

John Leeson, the 'voice' of K9, soon to have his own new series.

K9 proved an instant success on his first appearance on 8 October 1977 – although the production team had covered their options by recording two endings for *The Invisible Enemy*: one where the robot stayed with his creator, Professor Marius, and the other leaving with the Doctor. The decision whom he was to follow was never in doubt for long.

During the four years in which K9 was constantly rescuing the Doctor from all manner of dangerous predicaments, three different models were used – Marks I, II and III – all of which underwent regular changes in the Visual Effects department. Running the model over uneven surfaces was always a problem, sometimes having to be overcome by the use of tight camera angles. Tom Baker, whose feelings about K9 were ambivalent at best, particularly remembered when it was taken down to Brighton in 1980 for some location filming for *The Leisure Hive* by David Fisher and refused to move on the shingle beach. In the end it had to be pulled along by thin wires which Tom swears can be seen on the video!

When it was announced in October 1980 that K9 was to be dropped from the next series of *Doctor Who* because he was 'too clever at solving the Doctor's problems', the outcry was instantaneous. The BBC was deluged with letters of protest and the story made headlines in the national press. 'Not since the death of Dickens' Little Nell has the nation faced such a trauma,' reported the *Daily Express* which canvassed the opinions of outraged young viewers across the country. A 'Save K9 Campaign' was also launched by fans. Then in January 1981 a press release from the BBC said the dog was to have a new lease of life in a Christmas special, *K9 and Company*, written by Terence Dudley. In this, the robot was sent to Sarah Jane Smith as a present and helped her to battle against black magic and satanism in a small English village. Co-starring with Elisabeth Sladen were Bill Fraser (Commander Pollock) and Colin Jeavons (George Travey) both of whom had appeared in earlier *Doctor Who* stories. However, plans that this might turn into a series did not materialise, and K9 was only seen again in 1983 in *The Five Doctors*.

In 1997, however, Bob Baker teamed up with music producer Paul Tams in a bid to relaunch K9 as a 'radically redesigned dog for the nineties'. The updated dog will be able to hover and tilt his head to one side, and will have a new range of weapons to use against opponents. Conceptual artwork has already been produced by computer graphics designer, Rory McLeish, and, aided by a promotional showreel, Bob Baker hopes his mechanical pooch will be back on TV in the new decade.

Elisabeth Sladen and K9 on a press call in 1980 for *K9 and Company*.

The Dashing Young Doctor

Any visitor to the picturesque little village of Quainton in Buckinghamshire gets the distinct impression of stepping back in time, so well preserved are the fourteenth-century church, the redbrick almhouses with their Dutch gables, and the quaint village school with its rooftop bell to summon the pupils. The tower of a nineteenth-century windmill and the flower-covered cottages around the triangular village green enhance the feeling still more. The sensation had a particular significance for both the series and also its new Doctor, Peter Davison, when they visited the beauty spot in the autumn of 1981. For this was the Doctor's first location shoot on *Black Orchid* by Terence Dudley, a story that also marked the first truly historical adventure in the series since Patrick Troughton's *The Highlanders*, way back in 1966.

For once, even the TARDIS seemed in keeping on the platform of the little railway station on the edge of the village. The time period of the story was evidently the late 1920s, and the old blue police box looked as if it had been standing for years beside a sign stating that this was Cranleigh Halt on the GWR line – rather than having been put in place only that morning. Almost at once, a cloud of smoke blew up from the rail tracks, and as it cleared a figure dressed for cricket stepped from the box. The cameras rolled and Peter Davison had arrived.

This scene, shot on 12 October 1981, was, in fact, another example of the skill of the design team behind *Doctor Who*. For 'Cranleigh Halt', aka Quainton Station which stands some six miles from Aylesbury and has been disused for years, had been specially refurbished to look like a typical rural station of the twenties where the Doctor materialises and becomes

PETER DAVISON

ACTOR: Peter Davison (1951–)

TIME-SPAN: 1982–4

CHARACTERISTICS: Youthful, zealous and determined. A man whose neat appearance and open smile masked a steely resolve to fight all galactic tyranny with his own brand of intelligence and ingenuity. He gave a clean-nosed, public school appeal to the character.

APPEARANCE: An Edwardian cricketer to a tee, the Doctor might just have strolled off a cricket pitch and, in fact, retained his outfit unchanged during his three years. The cream-coloured Regency-styled long coat with red piping was complemented by red-striped, pyjama-like trousers. He also wore a V-neck cricket jumper and a white, open-necked shirt with red question marks stitched on to both collars. The Doctor's outfit was rounded off by a cream-coloured hat with a wide red band and a stick of celery on his lapel – the reason for which remained forever a mystery.

Peter Davison making his debut as the youthful Doctor in *Black Orchid* in October 1981. Also in the picture, taken at Blackhurst Park, East Sussex, are his three companions, Nyssa (Sarah Sutton), Adric (Matthew Waterhouse) and Tegan (Janet Fielding).

embroiled in a murder mystery at a local stately home that hides a terrible secret. Even the white steam from the departing train was an illusion created by a smoke machine just below the level of the platform.

Quainton, in fact, was one of several locations in Buckinghamshire used for the story of *Black Orchid* in which the Doctor turned detective to solve a series of grisly murders. It was in the village that I met Peter Davison on a bright autumn morning just a few days before his inaugural press call at Blackhurst Park in Withyham, East Sussex. This estate was also used as the stand-in for Cranleigh Hall where the killer referred to only as 'the Unknown' is finally exposed as the hideously disfigured son of the noble owner. When the story was broadcast the following year it was justifiably described by TV critics as combining the best elements of an Agatha Christie mystery with that of a Hammer horror film.

One of the features of Davison's era as the Doctor were the number of far-flung locations both in this country and abroad which were used during a comparatively short time. But there could have been nowhere more quintessentially English to talk to the gentlemanly new Time Lord – nor anywhere more convivial than the *Sportsman Inn*, with its head-high thatched eaves, where the cast and crew congregated at the end of the day's filming. Following this, Peter and the whole crew went on to film a cricket match sequence at Blackhurst Park where, despite the fact it was supposed to be taking place in high summer, everyone shivered in cold October winds!

Like most of his predecessors, Peter was somewhat surprised to have been offered the part by the producer, John Nathan-Turner, the previous year. 'I was sitting at home one night and John rang me to tell me that Tom Baker was leaving the series,' he recalled. 'How would you like to be the new "Doctor Who"? John asked me. Well, I had thought about perhaps being *in* the series at some time, but never playing the lead role. I thought I would be too young for it. But John was obviously serious and I thought, 'How can I possibly not do it?' I knew I would never forgive myself if I turned it down. Sandra, my wife, was also keen that I should do it – especially if she could play one of my companions!'

As Peter mulled over his decision, he could not help thinking back to his very first television appearance in 1975 in a Thames TV production called *The Tomorrow People* which at the time was being hyped as ITV's answer to *Doctor Who*. The series, created by Roger Price, was about a group of telepathic people who possess the power to teleport themselves from one place to another and save mankind from alien threats. Peter appeared in the story *A Man For Emily* by Roger Price playing Elmer, a 'space cowboy in a blond curly wig' who escapes to Earth from an alien spaceship, causes chaos and lands up in jail where he refuses to return to the ship. Playing his 'companion', the spoilt Emily, was Sandra Dickinson whom he would later marry. *Doctor Who*, however, was to prove worlds away from this saga of supermen and women which lasted for six years but never managed to match its BBC rival. (Interestingly, Nicholas Lyndhurst who became a star in *Only Fools and Horses* also got his break into television in this series in an episode entitled *Hitler's Last Stand*, again written by Roger Price, broadcast the following year.)

Tall, blond-haired Peter was born inauspiciously on Friday 13 April 1951 in Streatham, London – although bad luck has never dogged his

Peter Davison comforts Janet Fielding.

subsequent career. His schooldays at the Winston Churchill Secondary Modern School in Woking were undistinguished, he says, and he did not really shine at anything until he took part in a Rotary Club public speaking contest. In the past the contest had always been won by the local girls' or boys' grammar schools, but Peter was entered and wrote what he describes as 'a mad speech on philosophy – which I knew nothing about'. Nevertheless, he won, and his headmaster was so amazed he promptly suggested that he should go to a stage school.

It was good advice because Peter had always much preferred composing songs and tinkering with electronic things rather than doing his homework and the result, not surprisingly, was just one O level. Although his parents would have preferred him to go into banking, Peter was more inclined to try acting and prepared a couple more speeches. His nerve held again when he went for an interview at the Central School of Speech and Acting and he got a place 'by the skin of my teeth'.

After completing the course in 1972, Peter obtained his first job at the Nottingham Playhouse – and it almost became his last. 'I had only one speech,' he recalled later. 'I had to come on and tell the princess her father was dead and she was the queen – and I forgot it. I knew what the gist of it was – "Your dad's dead" – so I just said the first thing that came into my head and the whole cast burst out laughing. I just remember going back to my dressing room and thinking, "Well, that's it. I've failed." Fortunately, it wasn't. The next night there was no problem.'

He went on to spend a year with the Edinburgh Young Lyceum Company, followed this with a series of Shakespearean productions including *Two Gentlemen of Verona*, *Hamlet* and *A Midsummer Night's Dream*. His childhood interest in technology particularly attracted him towards television, and when he was offered the job on *The Tomorrow People* he took every opportunity to learn about the technical side of acting for TV. The experience excited him as well as standing him in good stead when television roles became the main thrust of his career.

Peter's first major role was as Tom Holland in *Love For Lydia* based on a story by H.E. Bates. This was followed by another series set in a rural idyll, *All Creatures Great and Small*. After playing the young vet, Tristan Farnon, for three series, he became a household name. By coincidence, also working on the programme was a production unit manager named John Nathan-Turner, who never forgot Peter's engaging performance and later decided he was the right man for *Doctor Who*.

Peter Davison had, in fact, been a viewer of the series since it started, and although he was aware of the media coverage of Tom Baker's departure he was not prepared for what happened on 4 November 1980 when it was announced he was taking over the role. For on the BBC's *Nine O'Clock News* he found himself sharing equal prominence with Ronald Reagan who had just been elected as the American president! When he recovered from the shock, he was happy to talk about his delight at getting the part and also give his considered opinions of his predecessors to the *Daily Mail*. They make interesting reading.

William Hartnell: 'There was something very mysterious about him. He was almost evil in a way, and certainly the most bad-tempered of all the Doctors. He was also the most forgetful, more like an absent-minded professor than the others.'

Patrick Troughton: 'Patrick was the muddler. He was always getting into a mess. Although he always won through in the end, a lot of the time it was more by accident than by design.'

Jon Pertwee: 'Funnily enough, being a comedian, he played the Doctor straighter than any of the other actors. The way he did it was almost like melodrama a lot of the time.'

Tom Baker: 'He was the most eccentric and he was certainly the most bizarre. But the great thing about Tom was his unpredictability. He kept you guessing because you never knew what he was going to do next.'

What to do next was, in fact, the very question that Peter faced when taking over from the long-established incumbent. Both he and John Nathan-Turner felt the humour might have gone a bit over the top with Tom Baker and now wanted to make the character a bit more heroic and youthful, though not infallible. As to his costume, Peter was intrigued by the idea that there was a 'clothes room' in the TARDIS and he could go in there and pick things off the peg. He fancied something vaguely to do with cricket (which is his favourite sport) and in getting his way, agreed to Nathan-Turner's suggestions that he should have highlights in his hair and wear a stick of celery in his lapel. Both became trademarks of the new Doctor.

A number of stories which Peter inherited for his first series had been written with Tom Baker in mind and changes had to be made almost on the move. He also had to get used to the three companions already in place played by Sarah Sutton, Janet Fielding and Matthew Waterhouse – and admitted later he was never very happy with the idea of them being basically

Peter Davison gets a lift from Sarah Sutton while filming *Castrovalva* (1982).

The Doctor with the series' most expensive 'prop', Concorde, at snowbound Heathrow Airport in January 1980 during the filming of *Timeflight*.

anti the Doctor in order to create a little tension. All four did work well together, however, until Adric was spectacularly killed off by a bomb and later replaced by the unpredictable schoolboy, Turlough (Mark Strickland, 1983–4) who had his own sinister agenda where the Doctor was concerned.

Sarah and Janet liked to jokingly refer to their roles at the time as 'the Doctor's harem' and Peter was asked about their relationship by the *Daily Mirror*. 'The golden rule is no hanky-panky,' he said. 'Originally the Doctor was a grandfather figure; then a favourite uncle. Now he is just a good friend to the girls.

'The Doctor has strict morals and each actor who plays him has a responsibility to maintain that tradition. The audience, especially the children, has to believe that men and women can be close friends sharing a home without sex. I am responsible for the Doctor's image off screen and it wouldn't do for me to be involved in any scandal. Fighting in pubs, throwing things at my wife – anything outrageous – is not for me.'

Peter has fond memories of two other location shoots he went on with the girls, the first in London at Heathrow Airport in January 1980 and the second, two years later, in Amsterdam in May 1982.

Timeflight by Peter Grimwade had as its centrepiece a British Airways Concorde which mysteriously disappears and has evidently been dragged back in time. Obviously it was absolutely crucial to show one of the aircraft in the story, but with the plane estimated to be worth a cool £30 million *a day* this would have made the location expenses for a single day's shooting a record for *Doctor Who* – indeed for *any* television programme. But thanks to an agreement made with BA and the British Airport Authorities, the series was loaned the supersonic aircraft for a day *free of charge* – the first time a fictional story had been given this facility. The contrast between the aircraft and the TARDIS when the machine was seen materialising beside it at Heathrow could not have been greater – though the Doctor maintains *his* means of transport is by far the faster.

'This was an amazing shoot,' Peter recalled. 'On the day we were supposed to film at Heathrow an absolute blizzard blew up and we had to film three days later when there was still snow on the ground and it was bitterly cold. That was quite a problem for all of us, especially Sarah and Janet keeping their long legs warm. I remember they got themselves togged up in thermal pants between takes and then took them off again ready for filming. There was a lot of laughing and joking while the girls struggled to get in and out of the pants without pulling off what they'd got underneath!'

After filming around Concorde, the crew also shot some footage in one of BA's passenger lounges and then returned to Studio 8 at the BBC Television Centre where a set had been built to recreate the area of Heathrow in prehistoric times. After the technical sophistication of the earlier scenes, Peter's one disappointment in this story in which the Master is ultimately discovered to have been responsible for an elaborate conjuring trick were the monsters which he described as 'just lumps of polystyrene'.

Peter himself got the chance to play a rather more realistic monster two years later when the programme went to Amsterdam for location shooting on *Arc of Infinity* by Johnny Byrne in which the embittered Time Lord, Omega (Stephen Thorne), last seen in *The Three Doctors* in 1972, returns to try and bond his anti-matter body with that of the Doctor. Early scenes were shot at Schiphol Airport and then the cast and crew moved on to film in the Muntplein town square and around a number of buildings in the Herenstraat and Singel streets. The Huis Frankendael and delightfully named Skinny Bridge were chosen for the grimmest moments of the story when Omega tries to take over the Doctor's body.

'We did this extraordinary bit of filming,' Peter says. 'I was playing two parts, the Doctor and Omega, as he was trying to turn into me. Because I was supposed to be decaying, they stuck me in a boiler suit with green latex and a mixture of glue, rice crispies and all sorts over my face. It took the make-up people hours to put on. Then with the camera crew out of sight, I had to run across Dam Square, which is pretty big and always crowded with people. They had no idea what was going on and just stood and stared. It wasn't easy for me, either, dodging all the cars and trams as I was running. We did that take four times – and then the BBC decided it was too horrific and it was cut!'

The confrontation between the two Time Lords was shot at the Lock gates just to the south of the Skinny Bridge with Peter playing both parts and having to make a quick costume change with crowds all around to watch the filming. He was particularly amused during one break at the canalside when a passer-by said, 'Good morning, Dr Herriot' under the mistaken impression that Peter was filming another episode for *All Creatures Great and Small* which was then running on Dutch TV! There were also a lot of amused faces when he hired a tandem and took Janet Fielding – both of them still in costume – on a ride around the city. He nicknamed his steed 'a bicycle made for Who'.

Arc of Infinity is, though, a landmark in the series' history for another quite different reason. A young actor named Colin Baker played one of the minor roles, Commander Maxil, and gave such an edge to the part that it stuck in the minds of everyone who saw it.

Like Tom Baker, Peter endeavoured to inject the odd joke or two into the script. Because of his fascination with technology he was not above having a bit of fun with the way he worked the console of the TARDIS. He was also keen that the storylines did not become stereotyped and the production values were kept high. Furthermore, he had already decided after a conversation with Patrick Troughton when he was given the role, that he was not going to remain for more than three seasons and would put everything he could into the role during that time.

One element of *Doctor Who* that did make him unhappy was the fact that despite the success of the series, money and schedules were always incredibly tight. Sometimes, he says, there was barely time to rehearse a scene before it had to be shot or the filming would run into extremely expensive overtime costs. This also meant that a number of special effects planned for certain stories had to be omitted because the budget could not afford them. Peter believes that some of the really hectic days must have been a bit like those experienced by television's earliest actors when programmes were transmitted 'live' and they, too, were ruled by the clock.

Making the anniversary special, *The Five Doctors* by Terrance Dicks, was also not without its problems of scripting, casting and filming. There was always a worry that the egos of the Doctors might clash – which Peter insists did *not* happen – as well as covering up the absence of Tom Baker who did not want to return to the show so soon and withdrew just before rehearsals were about to begin. It was also necessary to get a replacement for the late William Hartnell and in Richard Hurndall a perfect stand-in was found. (See *Four Doctors and a Dummy*.)

Terrance Dicks worked wonders juggling all the elements of the story, although the four Doctors all thought it was a shame they could not have appeared together at least once in the story. The location filming was done in familiar Welsh territory with the cast and crew staying in the little village of Maenturog where fans of the series had a field day collecting autographs. Despite all the changes and last-minute hitches which occurred in the making of *The Five Doctors* – as a much-thumbed and annotated copy of the script in my possession bears eloquent testimony – the story was a triumph for all the surviving Doctors and especially Peter

Davison. There are those who believe that had he gone on to do a fourth series after this, he might well have become the finest Doctor of all.

As it was, Peter decided to make the most of a further location shoot in Lanzarote in the Canary Islands in October 1983 where his penultimate story *Planet of Fire* by Peter Grimwade was filmed in October 1983. The story of another clash of wills between the Doctor and the Master on the divided planet of Sarn introduced a new companion – the first American, botany student Perpugilliam Brown (or Peri for short) played by Nicola Bryant (1983–6). Interestingly, it was Nicola's first TV role after leaving the Webber Douglas Academy and she brought an interesting connection to the series – her agent was Terry Carney, the husband of William Hartnell's daughter.

The same story also saw the last of the remarkable robot, Kamelion, which had made its debut in *The King's Demons* by Terence Dudley. The shape-shifting robot was intended to become a unique addition to the series before fate intervened. The robot was, in fact, a working animatronic prop controlled by a computer which meant that it could move, gesture, and make a variety of facial expressions. It had been designed by Richard Gregory and built by the Imagineering Special Effect Company. Such was the impact of Kamelion in Terence Dudley's story that it was decided to make the robot a permanent feature. Tragically, the computer specialist who had provided all the robot's software died suddenly in an accident and it was discovered that he had left virtually no documentation from which others could continue to work the machine and develop its potential. Kamelion's rather static performance in *Planet of Fire* – albeit with the addition of Gerald Flood's voice – was, in fact, his last.

By this time, Peter Davison had confirmed that this was to be his last season, too.

'My view of *Doctor Who* was that I was playing a part,' he says. 'But somehow you take on the mantle of the Doctor and a kind of instant charisma goes with the job. In the end, it became simply a matter of being obsessed about being typecast. Everything I had done before had been in three-year blocks and I was afraid that if I did a fourth, I'd end up doing a fifth, *ad infinitum*. So I decided it was time to go. I was quite relieved once I had made the decision, although there was always that little bit of uncertainty at the back of my mind as to whether I would work again.'

If Peter had any doubt about his own career, he was in no doubt about who would be taking over his role long before the announcement was

made. He has suggested on more than one occasion in interviews that he thinks that John Nathan-Turner 'in a kind of Truffaut-esque way' wanted to cast someone like himself in the part. Peter had also bumped into the producer with Colin Baker when both were huddled over drinks in a pub near the studios. That fact – and comments he recalled Baker making during the filming of *Arc of Infinity* that he fancied playing the Doctor – convinced Peter he was right. He was, of course.

Since leaving the series, Peter had attended a number of fan conventions and was lined up for a return in 1993 for an ill-fated thirtieth anniversary special to be called *The Dark Dimension* which would once again have reunited all the living Doctors up to and including Sylvester

A surprised Peter Davison is caught by Eamonn Andrews outside the TARDIS on 18 March 1982 for Thames Television's *This Is Your Life.*

McCoy. But despite a script being written and a director, Graeme Harper, being signed up, the special was never made. Instead, the anniversary was marked by *Dimensions in Time* for the BBC's *Children in Need* programme in 1993 in which Peter's role was confined to blowing up a Cyberman.

Peter Davison need not have feared about typecasting for since leaving *Doctor Who* he has worked regularly in the theatre, in films and on TV – a fitting recognition of his versatile talent. He remains satisfied with his achievements in the series, but sad about its current absence from the screen, though he does believe the idea is such a good one that it will come back.

During early 1998, while appearing in a new version of the classic thriller, *Dial M For Murder*, the tour brought Peter to Norwich's Theatre Royal where journalists were once again unable to resist asking a former Doctor what he felt about the series. With a typical smile he replied: 'I do feel I have managed to distance myself from the character now – but if I got to the age of sixty-five and somebody offered it to me then, I'd do it till I dropped. It's a great form of retirement – you just keep going until you keel over!'

Four Doctors and a Dummy

The idea of celebrating the Doctor's twentieth anniversary in November 1983 with a special one-off story, *The Five Doctors*, created not one but two headaches for producer John Nathan-Turner. Firstly, the original Doctor, William Hartnell, was dead; and, secondly, after believing that Tom Baker *would* appear in the story, the actor withdrew when pre-production was already under way. John solved the first problem by tracking down a look-alike actor, Richard Hurndall, to stand in for the first Doctor and for the second he borrowed a life-size wax model of Tom Baker from Madame Tussaud's in London for the press call to announce the project on 17 March 1983 at Haylings House in Denham, Buckinghamshire. (Tom is, in fact, the first and only person ever to have *two* likenesses in Madame Tussaud's: one his normal appearance as the Doctor and the other his 'cactus-covered' appearance in *Meglos* by John Flanagan and Andrew McCulloch (1980) caused by a skin infection that meant changes to the script *and* his features.) The producer was also able to include a 'live' Baker in the final story by using some unseen footage of the Doctor in Cambridge from the aborted Douglas Adams story, *Shada* (1979).

The choice of Richard Hurndall for the first Doctor was an inspired one. In fact, Nathan-Turner had seen the veteran actor on television in September 1981 in an episode of *Blake's 7* called *Assassin* by Rod Beacham. He was very struck by his likeness to Hartnell in the story about a mysterious killer who is threatening to kill the entire crew of the *Scorpio*. Richard jumped at the opportunity to appear in the special and told the press: 'I admired William Hartnell very much as an actor, and I have tried to play the role of the first Doctor as he would have done.'

Richard Gibbon Hurndall was born on 3 November 1910 at Darlington and after being educated at Scarborough College which first encouraged his interest in acting he joined RADA in 1927. Three years later he made his debut playing a footman in *A Pantomine Rehearsal* and during the next decade his good looks and forthright style made him a familiar figure in plays as diverse as *Charley's Aunt* to the works of Shakespeare. Like William Hartnell, he also appeared in several of Noel Coward's plays including a memorable *Private Lives*.

He took to television in its early days after the Second World War and gave fine performances in productions of *Philby, Burgess and Maclean*, *Love in a Cold Climate* and *Enemy at the Door*. Richard also became a familiar voice with the BBC Radio Drama Repertory Company from the late forties.

In the company of Troughton, Pertwee and Davison, he recreated the first Doctor so accurately in costume and long white wig that a stunned silence greeted his first emergence from Make Up – followed by a round of applause. Both Patrick Troughton and Jon Pertwee who had, of course, worked with Hartnell found his performance 'uncanny and brilliant'.

Sadly, Richard Hurndall died just a year later on 13 April 1984, aged 73, but already assured of a place in the legend of *Doctor Who* . . .

The Doctor Who Ran Out of Time

? The Doctor was flying. High up against a backdrop of stars, the Time Lord in his multicoloured jacket, striped trousers and spats was gliding not altogether comfortably backwards and forwards, holding hands with a lithe little figure in green who seemed to have stepped from the pages of a children's story book rather than another of the Doctor's adventures in space and time.

The setting was, in fact, far from the studios and locations where the stories of *Doctor Who* are usually filmed. It was the stage of the Aldwych Theatre off the Strand on the morning of 26 January 1986, and the 'flight' was to introduce the current Doctor, Colin Baker, and his new companion, Bonnie Langford, then starring at the theatre. She was soon to join the Doctor as computer programmer Melanie Bush (1986–7), heavily into aerobics and muesli, who would tease the Doctor about his attitude and his health. Their one-off act that morning in the Edwardian auditorium of the thousand-seater theatre was especially for the benefit of an invited audience of writers and journalists, myself included. It was a performance the like of which the handsome, ornate theatre had not seen before. It was also one that Colin Baker would never forget.

Colin had been hoisted aloft with Bonnie who was in costume for her leading role in *Peter Pan – The Musical* which was then nearing the end of its Christmas run. The little redhead, a song and dance star since her childhood, and still best known for playing the precocious Violet Elizabeth Bott in the *Just William* TV series, already had several weeks of experience flying around the stage. But for Colin it was a completely new sensation and one which would subsequently lead to rumours that he was

? COLIN BAKER

ACTOR: Colin Baker (1943–)

TIME-SPAN: 1984–6

CHARACTERISTICS: Brash, articulate and arrogant, but also very witty. Often spiky and verbose, his awful dress sense made him at first glance seem a rather ridiculous figure. Mostly clever enough to brazen his way out of the most difficult situations.

APPEARANCE: Dressed in a totally tasteless suit combining many different colours and patterns, no one could miss this Doctor. Although his long coat was similar in style to that of his predecessor, it combined panels of green and red check with similar ones of yellow, pink, purple and black, plus striped cuffs and enormous pockets! He also wore a dark-patterned waistcoat and white shirt and red squares down the front and the same red question marks on the collars. Under this collar hung a long turquoise necktie. His trousers were of yellow and black stripes, rounded off by red spats and green shoes.

The first Doctor to 'fly', Colin Baker, with co-star Bonnie Langford in January 1986.

overweight and was in danger of losing his role as the Doctor if he did not slim. In truth, it took all of his concentration to keep a smile on his face as he was swung about the stage suspended on one of the Kirby's Flying Ballet wires that was in everyday use in *Peter Pan*.

'I was wearing the harness under my costume,' Colin was to explain to me later, 'and it was a bloody great thing that pushed everything up and made me look a lot fatter. My hair had also been made up for the shoot in a bit of a hurry and it was so tightly curled that it made my head look like a great football. I know Bonnie was delighted with those pictures of us flying, but I thought they were dreadful. They made me look so fat and started all sorts of stories. In fact, it wasn't until I did the next story and got straight into the old costume that the people at the BBC were convinced that I *hadn't* put on pounds!'

Colin Baker has been equally frank about how he landed the part of the Time Lord in the first place. He says it all came about because of his tendency to show off. He remembers wringing every little bit out of the part of Commander Maxil in *Arc of Infinity* in order to catch the eye of the director, Ron Jones, and perhaps get more work. On camera he gave the part a strange, sinister quality that was impossible to ignore. In between waiting for shots, he also kept the rest of the cast and crew entertained with a series of impressions using the Commander's helmet of plumed feathers. Colin still jokingly refers to the hat as Esmeralda, 'because it looked like an excited chicken'.

Ron Jones never forgot the performance and is credited with having first suggested Colin Baker as a potential Doctor to producer John Nathan-Turner when Peter Davison announced he was leaving the series. What is beyond doubt is that Colin's infectious sense of humour and ability to entertain hard-bitten professionals gave him the edge over a number of other actors gossip said were being considered for the role. His only sadness today is that his tenure as the sixth Doctor was to end so unhappily . . .

Colin Baker was born in London on 8 June 1943, but moved to Manchester with his parents when he was just two years old. He spent the next twenty-one years in the city, and after leaving school, in deference to his father's wishes, trained to be a solicitor. In his spare time, however, Colin pursued his love of the theatre and joined several amateur dramatic societies. For five years he worked as an articled clerk before suddenly giving it all up. The reason was simple and poignant – his father had just suffered a stroke and Colin, worried that the same thing might happen to him, decided against spending his life in a career he did not really enjoy. So instead of sitting his finals in London, he went for an audition at the London Academy of Music and Dramatic Arts and secured a place. The decision is one he has never had cause to regret.

Colin left LAMDA in 1961 and after a period with a touring company and three years in repertory, he made his television debut in 1970. This came in the BBC's ground-breaking series, *Roads to Freedom*, based on three Jean-Paul Sartre novels of life, politics and defeat set in France between 1938–40. The production was the first drama marathon to include real-life characters including Daladier, Hitler and Chamberlain and starred Michael Bryant, Daniel Massey and Rosemary Leach. Colin played a rapist! His later work in the medium included a whole series of one-off performances ranging from a sensitive young poet in *Cousin Bette* to a villain in the police series, *Juliet Bravo*.

Public recognition came to Colin Baker when he landed the role of the scheming Paul Merroney in *The Brothers*, the BBC's long-running

The flamboyant
Doctor meets the
press with his first
companion, Peri
(Nicola Bryant), in
1984.

series in the seventies about a family in the trucking business dominated by their mother (Jean Anderson). For a time the Sunday night programme was required watching for millions of British viewers with Colin Baker the man they *all* loved to hate!

When *The Brothers* finished, Colin admits he was unable to get any work in television for five years, so identified had he become with the series. Instead he toured in a number of stage comedies and thrillers and worked in several movies including the futuristic story about a world of violence, *A Clockwork Orange* (1971), which its maker, Stanley Kubrick, has since banned from being reshown because he believes its influence to be too pervasive. In 1980, however, Colin took a step closer to *Doctor Who* when he landed a role in *Blake's 7*, the cult TV series created by Terry Nation. Colin appeared in the third season story, *City at the Edge of the World* by Chris Boucher. He played Babyon in a bizarre story about the opening of a strange vault. His co-star was Valentine Dyall whose name is, of course, also inextricably linked to *Doctor Who* as the Black Guardian.

Colin has said he was a watcher of *Doctor Who* since the days of William Hartnell — though he particularly admired the performance of Patrick Troughton and says it is always possible to tell the age of any fan of the programme by asking who is their favourite Doctor! The development of his own career meant he saw little of Jon Pertwee or Tom Baker in the role, but caught up again with Peter Davison through personal involvement. Each of the actors, he believes, has contributed something unique to the part. This made him determined to add another dimension when John Nathan-Turner offered him the role, beginning in *The Caves of Androzani* by the evergreen Robert Holmes, one of the most admired of all the series' scriptwriters. (See *Stories from Little Northover*.)

Just how daunting the task facing Colin would be was encapsulated in one newspaper's comment on his casting: 'Actor Colin Baker, once a J.R. Ewing-type television screen villain, is to take on the role of one of the small screen's most loved heroes, Doctor Who!'

He does, though, remember with delight one moment after filming the regeneration scene with Peter Davison. He returned home, swept open the door and declared to his wife, Marion: 'I am the Doctor!' She was quiet for just a moment. 'Oh, yes?' she replied. 'Well, could you take the rubbish out, please?' Those few down-to-earth words, he says, helped him to keep a sense of balance during the difficult times which followed.

Because of his long history of playing villains on TV, Colin at first visualised making his Doctor a rather dark figure in an austere black costume. John Nathan-Turner, on the other hand, fancied something quite the opposite: a Doctor who exemplified the height of bad taste. The result was the multicoloured suit which required several modifications before everyone was happy. Colin himself contributed the trademark cat badge on the lapel. He then gave life to a character who was a little more alien than his predecessors and certainly more erratic. In a nice tribute to his predecessors he often incorporated certain mannerisms they had used and then challenged fans to spot them.

'It's everybody's dream to play their hero, whether it is Lancelot or Biggles or Doctor Who because they are characters in modern mythology,' he was quoted as saying in March 1984 when making his first fully fledged appearance in *The Twin Dilemma* by Anthony Steven and Eric Saward. 'I always suspected it would be good fun. I feel almost as though the part was made for me – or I was made for the part.'

Initially, he found mustering the reserves of energy for the tight schedule the hardest thing to do. That and standing around in the cold and rain waiting to film scenes in the chalk and clay pits that have been so frequently used as alien landscapes in the series.

'When it is raining, it is all right for the crew – they can put wellies on,' he reminisced later about one of the stark realities of making a modern TV series. 'I have to walk around with plastic bags on my legs and keep wiping the mud from my shoes. And no matter how many thermals you're wearing, you're *freezing*.'

Although Colin has always maintained that *Doctor Who* would benefit from having more money spent on it, he has never wanted the series to compete with *Star Wars* or *Star Trek* in terms of special effects or lose its essentially English character – which, he believes, is one of the main reasons for its popularity in America.

The spring of 1984 also saw the first controversy during Colin's time when a report appeared in several national newspapers that the BBC were thinking of replacing the TARDIS with a more up-to-date machine as police boxes had long since disappeared from the British countryside and they meant nothing to young viewers. Whether the story was true or just a publicity stunt, a campaign was at once launched to save the time machine, attracting a number of letters to the *Radio Times*. 'Don't do it,' one reader, Katie Mallet, protested, 'the TARDIS is almost a national

institution!' The press also carried pictures of Colin standing outside the famous police box pleading with fans, 'Save My TARDIS!' Within a matter of weeks, the idea had been dropped and the time machine was said to be safe for another twenty years of travel.

Filming *The Two Doctors* with Patrick Troughton in August 1984 was one of the highlights of the series for Colin Baker.

For Colin Baker the highlight of 1984 came in August with the filming of *The Two Doctors*, again by Robert Holmes, which gave him the opportunity of working with his favourite Doctor, Patrick Troughton, not to mention an exotic location near Seville in Spain. For Nicola Bryant, still the Doctor's companion Peri, working with the two men made her the butt of as many jokes as her predecessor, Deborah Watling, had been subjected to – in particular one involving water.

For one scene, Colin had to splash water on Nicola's face in order to bring her round from being unconscious. It was to be the last take of the day, and director Peter Moffat was anxious to get it right the first time.

Although Nicola was quite evidently nervous – having already been teased several times by her co-stars – the scene went perfectly. But no one told her. Replaying the scene a second time, Colin threw a whole jug of water on the young girl, leaving her absolutely drenched. Unaware she had been fooled, Nicola struggled to get her lines out with a mouth full of water and it took her several moments to realise it had all been a joke.

Notwithstanding such pranks, Colin and Nicola did develop a close working relationship – although it was not always easy for her to keep a straight face when Colin and Patrick Troughton were both trying to put the most suggestive innuendos on certain lines of their dialogue. The fact that Holmes's typically comic script featured characters like Joinson Dastari (Laurence Payne), Chessene o' the Franzine Grig (Jacqueline Pearce), Marshal Stike (Clinton Greyn) and Shockeye (John Stratton) played right into the two actors' mischievous minds.

'There was an awful lot of joking between Pat and I on that Spanish shoot,' Colin says. 'We were both a bit badly behaved and took the piss out of each other unmercifully. I used to call him a geriatric and he got his own back by calling me "Fatty".'

In fact, Baker and Troughton had met each other before they worked in *The Two Doctors*, because Colin once shared a flat with David Troughton when both were young actors in London chasing girls, having a good time and grabbing any jobs they could find. When David later got married, Colin was his best man and met his father at the wedding. The pair very quickly realised they shared the same sense of humour, and working on *The Two Doctors* was an experience neither would have missed.

That high point of the autumn went sour for Colin and *Doctor Who* fans in general when it was announced on 27 February 1985 that the series was being taken off the air for eighteen months because the BBC could not afford the current cost of £100,000 for each fifty-minute episode. It was reported that the levels of violence in some of the stories had also become unacceptable and a major rethink of the programme was being ordered. The shockwaves for what might herald the end of the world's longest-running sf TV series were felt all over the world.

'John Nathan-Turner phoned me to tell me the news that it was being taken off before I read it in the newspapers,' Colin said later. 'It was fairly devastating. But my wife was just about to have a baby and that helped to put everything into perspective. We had lost our son, Jack, in a cot death, and news of the suspension came as Lucy was due to be born. It made me realise that a job is just a job. I was able to spend most of the time at home with her. The BBC effectively gave me paternity leave.'

The cancellation decision had been made by Michael Grade, the new Controller of BBC1, who had already dropped *Miss World*, *Superstars* and *The World's Strongest Man* from the schedules. The plan was defended by Bill Cotton, managing director of BBC Television who issued a press statement: 'The BBC has to live within its income. We are anxious to keep up the high standard of the production, and after considering a number of production options we decided we could not maintain every project.'

I was one of several people contacted by the press for a reaction to the news. The first was Stephen Cook of the *Guardian* who described me as '*Doctor Who's* official historian' and quoted me as being worried by the decision. 'What other programme could change the central actor and his character and still hold a magic grip over each new generation?' I said. '*Doctor Who* is unique – there will be a tremendous outcry to save it.' I also recalled that Mr Grade's last controversial decision – to interrupt the current run of *Dallas*, recently lost to ITV, so as to spoil the other network's plans for the next run of the soap – had been reversed as a result of public protests. During the rest of that day similar calls came in from all over the world, including one from the *Christchurch Press* in far away New Zealand, to whom I said, 'I'm astounded that the BBC has seen fit to axe its most popular product and I'm sure they will be hearing from a lot of the show's 110 million viewers in fifty-four countries.'

Colin Baker was just as horrified, but for much more personal reasons. 'The cancellation is very disappointing,' he said. 'The Doctor is a part I enjoy playing enormously and it's also my livelihood. I have a wife and children and a mortgage to pay, but I think it will be the end of one of the greatest traditions in TV if it is killed off.'

Patrick Troughton also spoke out on behalf of the show, telling the *Daily Telegraph* – which had been the first newspaper to break the news he was taking over from William Hartnell – that he thought there might be a hidden agenda behind the decision. 'It is possible the BBC is hoping there will be a public outcry about the series being too expensive for their resources. I would have thought most people will put two and two together and realise that what is in the minds of the Executives is a propaganda coup to support the Corporation's call for a higher licence fee.' (Curiously, the following day, the US *Doctor Who* fan club offered to raise $5 million 'if needed' to save the show.)

Although insiders at the BBC were quick to deny this theory, fans and the press kept up the pressure on the Corporation. The *Daily Star* launched a 'Save Doctor Who' campaign and recruited a group of famous fans including Justin Hayward, Faith Brown, Sally Thomsett, Richie Pitts and Warren Cann to form a band, Who Cares, and make a record with Colin and Nicola Bryant called 'Doctor In Distress' – the proceeds all going to aid Cancer Relief.

The result of the furore was another statement from Bill Cotton on 1 March: '*Doctor Who* will be back on the air in 1986,' he said. 'We are also going back to the old tradition and having twenty-five-minute programmes rather than the forty-five-minute version which we think is what the public wants. We appreciate the passionate support of the fans around the world. We ask them to be a little patient while we get the Doctor back on to familiar rails. I am confident that *Doctor Who* has a great future.'

With the benefit of hindsight, Colin Baker admits that he was obviously in a difficult position with the most to lose if the programme was axed and he had to be careful what he said about his employers. He also felt there was less incentive for Michael Grade to continue with a programme he had inherited, but contests the Controller's statement that the viewing figures were 'disappointing'. Baker maintains that the figures between seven and nine million were better than any equivalent pro-gramme being put out at the same time. He has always agreed that public taste towards violence must be taken into account, but that over the years this attitude has changed and cited the show which was then being shown opposite *Doctor Who* on ITV – *The A-Team*, a mélange of violent action with a whole group of gun-wielding characters.

'I don't think *Doctor Who* was ever too violent,' he says. 'If we do show violence on television, then let it be honest. If somebody is punched, let it look as though it hurts. That is the only way we are ever going to get an anti-violence message across to youngsters.'

Colin Baker was not the only person to see the irony of the storyline for the entire 1986 season – the fourteen-parter, *The Trial of a Time Lord* written by Robert Holmes, Philip Martin and Pip and Jane Baker. In this, the Doctor – like the series itself – was in the dock: the Time Lord charged with interfering in planetary affairs before a court of his peers. He was cross-examined by a Time Lord, the Valeyard (Michael Jayston), who was revealed in the final dramatic moments of the story to actually be a future incarnation of the Doctor *himself*.

Following the introduction of Bonnie Langford as the Doctor's new companion at the Aldwych, another open day for the press was held on 10 April 1986 during location filming for the first episode of the 'trial' entitled *The Mysterious Planet* by Robert Holmes. In order to depict a future Earth where a holocaust has forced the remaining inhabitants to adopt a primitive lifestyle, the production team chose to film at an Iron Age Village at Butser Hill near Petersfield in Hampshire. Leading the co-stars was the ebullient Joan Sims, as Katryca, warrior queen of the Tribe of the Free, who brandished a pair of guns and proved a favourite with all the photographers when she posed in front of one of the ancient village huts!

'Joan Sims was just wonderful,' Colin recalls. 'She told me it was such a change to wear a bizarre costume and that glorious red wig. She thought that some people might not even recognise her. It is so easy to say that she just does the *Carry On* films, but she's actually an *actress*.'

Joan Sims – aka the warrior queen Katryca – posing for the press at the Iron Age Village in Petersfield in April 1986 during filming of *The Mysterious Planet.*

Among the other familiar names who appeared in *The Trial of a Time Lord* were Brian Blessed (as King Yrcanos), Honor Blackman (Professor Lasky) and Michael Craig (Commodore Travers).

With filming completed, *Doctor Who* returned to TV screens on 6 September 1986. *Today* newspaper commented, 'If the Doctor is found guilty, the sentence is death. And if the show is too violent or too tired, that sentence may well be carried out by Michael Grade.' Prophetic words indeed, because when the series ended on Saturday 6 December, its audience had peaked at five-and-a-half million viewers. On Thursday 19 December, the BBC announced that Colin Baker was leaving the series. What had occurred in the intervening two weeks is now a part of *Doctor Who* rumour and legend.

The morning papers of 19 December said that Colin had 'angrily' resigned from his starring role and was not prepared to accept an offer of four episodes in the next series to facilitate the regeneration of his successor. His agent, Barry Burnett, issued a statement which said simply, 'Colin is sorry and disappointed to be leaving a part he loved.'

There the story might well have ended, but for a front-page headline in the *Sun* of Monday 5 January 1987 which announced: '*Doctor Who Blasts Off! Beeb Boss Grade is just a coward, says sacked Colin Baker*'. The paper promised further revelations on the following two days during the course of which it was alleged that Michael Grade had 'slagged off' the series in public, 'backed out' of meeting Colin Baker face to face to tell him why he was being sacked, and 'insulted' millions of loyal fans. Most contentiously of all – in the second article – it was stated that sacking Baker 'Will Hit Cot Death Cash'. The articles were emotive and gave the impression that Colin was furious at the way the whole matter had been handled. In an attempt to get both sides of the story after the dust had settled I wrote to Michael Grade eight months later inviting him to put his side of the story.

The reply was terse and to the point: 'Thank you for your letter of September 23,' he wrote. 'I regret I am unable to help you, but thank you for asking.' The letter was signed, 'Yours sincerely, Michael Grade'.

Colin Baker has, however, subsequently helped to put the record straight and admitted that although Michael Grade was 'never particularly kind to me', he has 'no axe to grind' with him. It was in November 1986, he said, that John Nathan-Turner rang him with the news that although Michael Grade was authorising a new series of *Doctor Who*, the proviso was that a

new Doctor must be cast. Colin had played the role for three years and that was felt to be enough. Although Nathan-Turner pointed out that Baker had, in fact, only appeared in the show for one-and-a-half seasons, Grade was adamant. Colin, for his part, was not prepared to sign for four more episodes as this would lose him more than six months' acting work elsewhere.

In happier days: Colin Baker and *Doctor Who* producer, John Nathan-Turner.

'I never really took personal umbrage at what happened,' he says now. 'It was just an irritant in the same way as if a headmaster at school was to say that a holiday had been cancelled. It makes you feel a bit cross.'

He had, he admitted, a secret ambition to beat Tom Baker's record of seven years in the role, and had certainly been prepared to commit himself to three or even four years unlike his predecessor. Colin stands by his performance as the Doctor, and argues with those who feel he might have done more with the part by insisting he could only do what the scripts and directors allowed.

Of the *Sun* series of articles, Colin admits that he was paid, but claims that some of his more controversial quotes were taken out of context and then re-edited to suit the newspaper. He certainly did *not* infer that his leaving *Doctor Who* would deprive the Cot Death Foundation of money and says he has received an apology from the newspaper for this.

Colin wasted no time in taking up other offers of work, and went on a six-month tour with the mystery thriller, *Corpse*. He has also now branched out into directing, reading short stories for talking tapes, and composing music for pantomimes. He likes writing, too, and as well as a column in his local paper, the *Bucks Free Press*, creates short stories of romance, comedy and horror which he publishes under a pen-name. Deeply interested in the education of his four daughters, he also serves as a governor at a school not far from his lovely 200-year-old cottage home at Cadmore End near High Wycombe, Buckinghamshire.

Although he has done less television work – his most recent appearance was in *Casualty* (1997) – Colin Baker has maintained his connections with *Doctor Who* by attending fan conventions, appearing in the *Children In Need* skit, and successfully taking over the lead in the new stage production of *The Ultimate Adventure*, originally written for Jon Pertwee.

Time has mellowed the sixth Doctor and speaking recently he said, 'I have very happy memories of the series. It was like being paid to play cowboys and Indians. I really enjoyed playing the Doctor because it meant that the working atmosphere was, to a large extent, dictated by me. There aren't many really difficult people in the business, but if you do come across someone who is difficult, it can be hell. I was determined that everyone who came into the show should have a good time – and we did. It was hard work and sometimes you had to hang around for hours while Special Effects wielded the staple gun. But love him or hate him, my Doctor was *my* Doctor.'

Tales from Little Northover

One of my happiest memories of *Doctor Who* was my friendship and correspondence with Robert Holmes, probably the most respected and popular scriptwriter for the series. He was also highly influential as the programme's script editor from 1974 to 1977. Bob's association with the series extended from the days of Patrick Troughton right through to Colin Baker, and his work ranged from stories of high adventure to almost slapstick comedy. He it was who mounted a strong defence against those who claimed the programme was violent, and was featured in a famous *Daily Express* interview by Jean Rook entitled, 'Who do you think you are, scaring my innocent child?' He was the first writer invited to script the anniversary story, *The Five Doctors*, and it was a source of disappointment to him right up to the day of his death in 1986 that he was unable to undertake this job. Bob worked from his delightful home, Little Northover at Akeley in Buckinghamshire, and would often greet phonecallers with a fruity countryman's rendition of the name of the local exchange, 'Lillingstone Dayrell', for which he had a seemingly endless number of variations. We wrote to each other regularly when he was helping me with reminiscences for my earlier books about *Doctor Who*, and I have chosen four typical extracts from letters written by him in 1985 which will, I hope, provide a reminder of the wonderful sense of humour of this much-loved man who played such an integral part in the show's enduring success.

I will be happy to write something for your new book. As you will know, nothing funny happens while you spend most of your time staring at a typewriter. But I may dredge up an amusing anecdote or two from my days as the show's script editor. I hope there is no rush, because I am stuck – operative word – in the middle of a *Bergerac* at the moment . . .

12 July

You suggest I write something about *The Two Doctors*. As a matter of fact, I didn't have too much to do with that show, although I did attend the read through. On one of the hottest days of 1984 we crammed ourselves into a sudorific dog-kennel in a BBC dungeon. It was a day for sitting with one's feet in the fridge and thinking cool thoughts. I felt sorry for the actors who were due to depart for Spain. If it was like this in London they were probably already frying bulls on the pavements of Seville.

You know actors have dirtier minds than writers and can find filth in the most innocuous lines. Colin Baker started it. 'Look at this pretty thing,' he says. 'See how it swings . . . backwards and forwards, forwards and backwards . . .' There is a ribald laugh from the cast. Down the table Patrick Troughton is chuckling with his friend, Frazer Hines. Patrick can be funny, too. He can milk a line for its fourth *entendre*. He once explained to me that it's his way of getting all the giggles out of his system before beginning the serious acting . . .

4 August

Ere the stamp was dry on the missive I sent you yesterday than I remembered I had left uncorrected an elementary boo-boo. Somewhere about the middle of the piece I was chuntering on, in sub-Wodehousian fashion, about my teeth and mentioned that I could use them to send semaphore messages. As all old Boy Scouts should know, semaphore is flags. What I really meant to say was, 'On a sunny day I can send heliograph messages at ranges up to ten miles.'

Later, towards the end, I refer (actually, to one of my oldest friends in the business) as an 'irredeemable scoundrel'. Thinking about it, while 'irredeemable' is not wrong the word has a mainly monetary connotation. In the particular context, 'unredeemable' is a better choice. It is this attention to detail that has got me where I am today. Nowhere.

14 September

The much-lamented scriptwriter Robert Holmes, photographed by Stephen Payne.

Last week I had the flu – again – or some other related virus. Unable to sleep because of my aching bones I lay awake thinking of things I'd written and things I ought to write and eventually I had one of those dark thoughts that pop into one's mind at 2 a.m. Can Jacqueline Pearce have us for libel? My line about her, 'who obviously knows a pretty thing when she sees one' is comment and could, I think, be held to apply to the lady's character. In the *Doctor Who Cookbook* she claimed her ambition is to publish her collection of erotic verse and from what I know of her – working hard at her image as a *femme fatale* – she is not likely to be distressed. However, someone else might drop the idea into her mind. I have noticed, as I'm sure you have, that nobody is so sensitive as a litigant with unearned income in sight.

Anyway, as I dropped off around 3 a.m., this bowed and penitent hack, having lost his house as part of the out-of-court settlement, was being chased down the Strand by stone-throwing members of the Jacqueline Pearce Fan Club. I don't know what happened to you. I think you ran down towards the river where they probably threw you in.

28 October

Curtain Call for the Entertainer

? Almost a quarter of a century had passed since the TARDIS had last been seen in a very similar London neighbourhood. *That* day had marked the first appearance of the famous police box; but now, once again, the familiar figure of the Doctor was emerging through the doors: shorter, younger, more jaunty, certainly, but still undeniably the self-same Time Traveller. It was all those years ago, in fact, since his first 'self' had stepped out into a London street in the story of *An Unearthly Child* and the odyssey had begun. The only difference was that this was June 1989 and the place Medway Parade, just off Western Avenue, Perivale, and not Totter's Lane in Studio 'D' at Lime Grove in September 1963. The Doctor now was Sylvester McCoy and not William Hartnell.

Although Perivale and Lime Grove are less than five miles apart, in the intervening years since the first show, *Doctor Who* had become established as a cult favourite, and the Time Lord one of TV's favourite heroes. However, unbeknownst to anyone in Perivale that day, there was a portent about the location shooting for *Survival* by Rona Munro. For it was to prove the last story to be transmitted in the series made in England . . . for the time being. Few titles could have read more like an epitaph.

Not that there was any lack of good humour in Western Avenue on that June day – that was not the style of Sylvester McCoy's Doctor. For he had been joined on the day's shooting by two of Britain's leading comedians, Hale and Pace, appearing in cameo roles as Harvey and Len, two helpful souls in a supermarket who give the Doctor some advice on cat food. The TARDIS had landed in Perivale, the home of the Doctor's latest companion, the teenage waitress Ace (Sophie Aldred, 1987–9), to

SYLVESTER McCOY

ACTOR: **Sylvester McCoy (1943–)**

TIME-SPAN: **1987–9**

CHARACTERISTICS: **Quick-witted, intelligent and totally opposed to violence, he has a sense of wonder and a nice line in irony. A man who sees the follies of human beings – and also his own. He has an innocence about him and an ability to wander into dangerous situations which he should perhaps foresee. He also has a passion for minutiae and because he dislikes authority is regarded as something of a rebel.**

APPEARANCE: **Less outlandish than his immediate predecessors, the Doctor has something of the Edwardian professor about him; a man who could walk down any street without being considered too eccentric. His linen jacket has baggy pockets full of paraphernalia which somehow matches his tweedy check trousers – held up by red braces – and two-tone shoes. The colourful pullover covered in question marks offsets the Doctor's soft shirt and Paisley scarf. He also carries several timepieces – including a fob watch – and is never seen without his two trademarks: a panama hat with turned-up brim and umbrella with a red question mark for the handle.**

Sylvester McCoy made his debut as the Doctor for the benefit of the press in March 1987 with Bonnie Langford.

find that most of her friends had gone missing and some strange cheetah-like creatures were busy hunting down human beings. It would transpire that the Master was once again the controlling force behind the creatures who are slowly turning the whole world feline.

'Buying cat food must be one of the strangest things the Doctor has ever had to do,' Sylvester joked on the set, as he juggled with a couple of tins. 'It is a bit of a giggle, too, having Hale and Pace giving advice on cat food after all the trouble they've been in recently about their "cat in the microwave" joke!'

In fact the two comedians, formerly PE teachers who became famous playing a pair of hard-faced night club bouncers, Ron and Ron, had only just returned from the Montreaux Festival where they had been voted the top comics in Europe for their show – which also featured the notorious microwave sketch. Both were still a bit amazed that such an obvious joke could have been taken seriously and provoked such an outcry.

There were, in fact, a number of interesting parallels to be spotted between *Survival* and William Hartnell's debut story 25 years before. Once again the TARDIS was flying with all the audio and visual effects that had made its first appearance so stunning. Sylvester McCoy, like his original self, was becoming increasingly agitated and unstable during the story, while in Sophie Aldred, the Doctor had a companion in the same tradition as Carole Ann Ford, the fifteen-year-old from Coal Hill School. Carole was then twenty-two and married with a three-year-old daughter, while Sophie was twenty-six playing a sixteen-year-old.

'Although I never saw William Hartnell at the time he was in the series, I have seen some of his performances on video and I like that crabbiness and bad-temperedness,' Sylvester explains. 'But you have to remember that the Doctors are all the same person. *We're* not the same person, *he* is. In fact, when I first approached the role I thought it would be nice to get bits of each Doctor in my character because there is a kind of logical sense to that. It's the bit of Hartnell that makes me crabby every now and then.'

This desire to make the character entertaining was always uppermost in McCoy's attitude to his Doctor – and he employed many of the elements from his own exotic career in just about everything from opera to musicals and comedy to underpin the figure of the Time Lord. The appearance of several top comedians like Hale and Pace during Sylvester's

three seasons in the role also gave it a distinctive flavour all its own. The sum total marked a considerable achievement for a man who had a difficult childhood and survived a number of ups and downs in his working life – all of which he discussed frankly with me over dinner in a restaurant in the heart of London's theatreland where he has so often appeared.

Sylvester McCoy was born Percy Kent-Smith in Dunoon, Argyllshire on 20 August 1943. He never saw his father, a Londoner from Pimlico, who had met his mother while serving as an acting petty officer in the Royal Navy. Within six weeks of meeting, the couple were married, and after a two-week honeymoon in Ayrshire, his father returned to sea on a submarine which was soon afterwards blown up in the Mediterranean. He was just 23 and his new wife was already carrying their son. According to Sylvester, his mother never got over the trauma of her husband's tragic death and required medical treatment for the rest of her life.

Following his father's death, Sylvester and his mother went to live with an uncle in Dublin, where he remembers being very lonely and often hearing his mother crying for her lost husband. Later they returned to Scotland and the little boy was mainly brought up by his grandmother and other relatives. His mother, who was a heavy smoker, finally died of cancer.

While he was still at school, Sylvester made a decision that very nearly put him on the same path as his predecessor, Tom Baker. He was so keen on a suggestion made by a visiting clergyman that the priesthood might be the calling for him, he says, that he promptly went to Aberdeen and trained there for the ministry until he was 16. By then – like Baker before him – he had grown less sure he *had* a vocation for the church, and decided to leave and go to London. Here he worked for an insurance company in the city until it went bankrupt, enjoyed a period as a hippy, and then managed to get himself a job in the box office of the Roundhouse Theatre in North London – the only reason for this being, he says, because he was able to count! It was here that a chance meeting with the actor Brian Murphy, later to become a star of the hit TV series *George and Mildred*, changed his life.

'Brian was collecting the tickets and assumed that like him I was an out-of-work actor,' Sylvester recalls. 'A producer happened to come into the Roundhouse looking for someone to replace an actor who had let him down at the last minute for a roadshow. Brian told him, "The guy in

the box office is completely out of his head – he's just what you need." That's how I found myself travelling round the countryside doing all sorts of crazy sketches.'

The producer was the legendary Ken Campbell and it was on his *Roadshow* that Sylvester began to develop his talent as an entertainer. Another member of the same cast also destined for stardom was Bob Hoskins – and both men still remember their tours throughout the UK and Europe with the greatest affection.

Sylvester, in fact, has a fund of hilarious stories to tell about his madcap days with the *Roadshow* – one of which was to be widely featured when it was announced in the press that he was to be the new Doctor. At the time, he was appearing at the Theatre Royal in Stratford, East London in a Houdini sketch which involved escaping from a sack. At that early stage of his career, McCoy was still wearing the beard and long hair fashionable among hippies. He performed the escape trick wearing nothing but a mock ferret covering his midriff.

'The trouble was that on this particular night all the struggling to get out of the sack caused the ferret to come off,' says Sylvester, 'so when I appeared on stage I was stark naked! It did raise a few eyebrows, but nudity was all part of the scene in those days.'

Among the other madcap stunts in his repertoire were driving a three inch nail through his nose, putting a *live* ferret down his trousers, and performing as the 'Human Bomb'. The trouble with this act, he remembers, was that the bombs had a tendency to explode downwards burning his stomach.

The very variety of the roles he played for Ken Campbell gave Sylvester McCoy plenty of encouragement to expand his career. His later work included a number of Shakespearean productions, a dame in pantomime, and a wonderful period with the Welsh Opera Company. He was also Renfield in *Dracula* at the Lyric, Hammersmith, and Samuel in *Pirates of Penzance* at Drury Lane in which he co-starred with Bonnie Langford, later to be his first companion in *Doctor Who*. He also gave remarkable impersonations of two of his comedy heroes, Buster Keaton and Stan Laurel in specially written shows, *Buster's Last Stand*

Sylvester McCoy delighted in clowning for the press at his photo calls.

and *Gone With Hardy*. Both of these monologues focused on the sadness behind the smiles of the two men's lives. The performances all helped Sylvester to develop the feeling for comedy, drama and pathos which he later incorporated into his performance as the Doctor.

Sylvester took just as naturally to television. He appeared in *Starstrider* (Granada), *Number 73* (TVS) and as Birdie Bowers in *Last Place on Earth* (Central), as well as making a name for himself on several popular children's programmes including *Tiswas, Jigsaw, Vision On* and *Eureka* – the last two produced by Clive Doig who would later be influential in getting him the star part in *Doctor Who*. In fact, the Doctor was a role he had fancied playing for a number of years, and as soon as news of Colin Baker's departure hit the showbusiness grapevine, Sylvester was on the phone to his agent, Brian Wheeler.

'I suggested he call John Nathan-Turner,' McCoy remembers, 'but I didn't hear what happened until later. Apparently as soon as John had finished talking to my agent and put the phone down, he got another call. It was from Clive Doig and during their chat he suggested me for the part of the Doctor. "Are you two in cahoots?" John asked him. "No, no," Clive insisted as the previous conversation was explained to him, "it's just that I heard the news about Colin and I think you should see this man." So that got him interested and he came to see me at the National where I was appearing in *The Pied Piper*. The part had been specially written for me and it could almost have been an audition piece for the series.'

As Sylvester gambolled about the stage with fifty children following happily in his wake, John Nathan-Turner may well have been reminded of Patrick Troughton's Doctor. Curiously, too, Troughton was McCoy's favourite Doctor, especially because of his ability to mix humour and horror. As it was, the producer and actor met and after a discussion about the role, McCoy played two audition scenes with Janet Fielding written by the series' new script editor, Andrew Cartmel. One had him portraying the sadness of parting from a companion, the other a confrontation with an evil enemy.

Although at this moment in time nothing had been finalised about how Sylvester McCoy would play the Doctor – or even what his appearance would be like – he was so impressive that he was offered the job. He accepted without a moment's hesitation. But what happened next was even more extraordinary.

On 2 March 1987, the BBC Press Office announced that McCoy was to be the new Doctor. The news immediately prompted a headline in the London *Evening Standard*: *The Ferret Man is New Doctor Who* with the paper reporting that his previous major claim to fame was 'for holding the world record for stuffing a ferret down his trousers'. The Doctor Who Appreciation Society were also quoted in the same story as saying the fans would have preferred a better-known actor in the role.

'As you know,' Sylvester said to me later, 'I had done a lot of acting before, but there I was being greeted as "Sylvester Who?" The only thing they mentioned was the ferrets-down-the-trousers stunt. I was a little annoyed because the press just hadn't done their homework. I also didn't like fans judging me even before they had seen me. I just couldn't understand that. I told one of them that they shouldn't call themselves fans but the Doctor Who Critics' Society. You're knocking the programme so much, I said, you are going to put a nail in its coffin. People become fans for different reasons – they see different things and like what they see. So when it's not your programme, please leave, don't hang around and try to destroy it.'

These were to prove prophetic words indeed, but at the time Sylvester was keener on emphasising the positive side of the casting as he saw it. 'There is certainly something to be said coming to a famous part as a so-called unknown, because if you make a success of it everyone sits up and takes notice. It helps you after *Doctor Who* – because there *does* seem to be life after the series.'

Whether some considered him an 'unknown' or not, the following weekend Sylvester found sacks of fan mail beginning to arrive at his London home on Haverstock Hill in Hampstead which he shares with his wife, Agnes, and teenage sons, Sam and Joe. Most of the letters congratulated him on landing the role – *and* gave him advice on how to play the part. The writers suggested just about every way possible from a limp to a lisp, he recalls, and one even recommended that he dressed up in a magician's cloak. Interestingly, quite a number of the letters were postmarked 'USA', which gave Sylvester an immediate idea of just how world-wide was the interest in the series. Then, within the week, he found out all about it at first hand when he was flown to Atlanta, Georgia, to attend a major American *Doctor Who* convention.

'The fans in the States were amazing,' he later told his local paper, the *Hampstead and Highgate Express*. 'They all came dressed as their favourite Doctor or monster. I had to host a question-and-answer session, but they all knew more than me. So I had to get the audience to come up with the answers. It's amazing the way as the Doctor you can tap into all those years of adulation. It's a kind of instant love. You crack a joke and everyone bursts out laughing even if the joke isn't funny. I suppose it's an actor's dream.'

Later that same month Sylvester went back again to a second convention in Washington which coincided with the tragic death of Patrick Troughton in Georgia. 'It was such a sad moment for me,' he said on his return to London, 'because he was my favourite Doctor. And here was I just about to take over the role and I would never have a chance to meet him.'

This unhappy coincidence made Sylvester, if anything, even more determined to make his Doctor fresh and memorable, though as yet he was still not sure *how*.

'I am a very instinctive kind of actor,' he explains. 'I certainly had ideas in my mind while I was discussing the part, but they really didn't start to come together until I received the first scripts, got into the costume and then into the studios. However, I was involved in the process of picking the Doctor's outfit. The hat was exactly the same one I wore to the interview. In fact, John gave me the part because he liked the hat. "Well, if you want the hat, I go with it," I told him. We did try the idea of having a four-eyed Doctor as I normally wear glasses, but decided against this because my eyes could be seen more clearly without them. The umbrella with the red question mark handle was my own idea because I thought it would be a very useful thing to use in cliff-hanging episodes.

'I decided that the Doctor was a man who clearly loved the Earth, and therefore humanity. He doesn't like authority because authority has to prove its worth. Just because it *is* authority, it shouldn't be accepted. It should be questioned – and the Doctor does that and it gets him into trouble. He is a mixture of all sorts of things and has strengths and weaknesses, which are also interesting from an actor's point of view.'

Sylvester would, he says, have liked to take the Doctor back into the past during his tenure to see what was actually happening at any given moment, but was told that historical stories had proved not to be popular with viewers.

Because Colin Baker had refused to appear in the regeneration of the new Doctor, Sylvester was forced to play this scene on his own when production began again on the series in April 1987. It was the first time this had occurred in the quarter of a century *Doctor Who* had been running.

'It was not an easy thing to do,' he recalls. 'I was flung face down at the beginning of the story wearing Colin's costume and a curly wig. I thought I looked like Harpo Marx. Then as I was turned over there was a flash of my face, and when I saw this later I was surprised at how like Colin I looked. After that the picture went all funny and when it returned to normal I was me!'

The person who 'turned over' the new Doctor was Kate O'Mara returning to the series to give it a flying start as the villainous Rani in *Time and the Rani* by Pip and Jane Baker. Sylvester McCoy says he was a bit nervous about playing opposite the *Dynasty* star in his first episode, but found her 'delectable and wonderful' to work with – not to mention patient, as their first studio session together lasted for almost twelve hours. Having Bonnie Langford in the cast with whom he had worked previously was an added bonus and he very quickly felt a sense of being part of a well-established tradition. The fact that the director for the first story was Andrew Morgan who had supervised his screen test was the icing on the cake.

Sylvester's debut was warmly greeted by the public, too. A series of letters appeared in the *Radio Times* under the heading, 'New Doctor Who is the real McCoy!' Michael Daly from London summed up the consensus of opinion when he wrote, 'Sylvester McCoy promises to be the best Doctor yet . . . my only gripe is that the series is up against *Coronation Street* in the ratings battle.'

In the second story, *Paradise Towers* by Stephen Wyatt, Sylvester co-starred with Richard Briers playing his first ever TV role as a villain – the dastardly, Hitler-moustached Chief Caretaker who feeds people to his pet monster. The futuristic world of Paradise Towers complete with a huge housing block, long streets, an overhead gantry and town square was specially built at Television Centre. Brenda Bruce and Elizabeth Spriggs appearing as two sinister old conspirators made the story even more watchable. Another top comedian, Ken Dodd, was lined up for the third story, *Delta and the Bannermen* by Malcolm Kohl, which again Sylvester enjoyed making, most of it filmed on location in Wales. (See *The Doctor and the Diddyman*).

The final story of Sylvester's first season (the twenty-fourth, in fact), *Dragonfire* by Ian Briggs, saw the departure of Bonnie Langford to be replaced by the street-wise young Ace. A tough and resolute character who delighted in calling the Doctor 'Professor', she represented a dream–come–true for Sophie Aldred, a presenter on the children's TV show, *Corners*, who had been a fan of the series since the days of Jon Pertwee. Unfortunately, she told the *Radio Times* on joining the series, her rapidly escalating fear of the Cybermen had caused her to spend most Saturday tea-times behind the sofa. 'In the end my mum banned me from watching it,' she said. 'Now I have the chance to get my own back on the Cybermen!'

The second season marking the silver anniversary of *Doctor Who* began appropriately with the return of the Doctor's oldest adversaries in *Remembrance of the Daleks* by Ben Aaronovitch. In this, Sylvester and Ace were locked in a race to find the immensely powerful Hand of Omega which is also being sought by the Daleks. The filming took place in London during April 1988, and the shooting of a Dalek battle scene proved so explosive that it resulted in the emergency services being

The Doctor confronted by the evil Chief Caretaker – Richard Briers playing his first TV role as a baddie – in *Paradise Towers* (1987).

called and made the pages of the national press the following day. The incident happened in Theed Street, near Waterloo Station, when an explosion under a railway bridge set off all the car alarms in the vicinity and was so loud it was heard right across the city.

Those other formidable villains, the Cybermen, also returned much to Sophie Aldred's delight in the anniversary story *Silver Nemesis* by Kevin Clark, the first episode of which was broadcast on 23 November 1988. Again much of the story was filmed on location during June, with the Greenwich Gas Works in London and Arundel Castle, Sussex being used as the background against which the Doctor finally outsmarts the Cybermen in their quest to seize a powerful Gallifreyan statue.

What would prove to be the third and final season for Sylvester McCoy started with *Battlefield* by Ben Aaronovitch, in which two old favourites returned: the Brigadier (Nicholas Courtney) and Jean Marsh who had first appeared with William Hartnell in *The Crusade* (1965) playing Joanna, the sister of Richard the Lionheart. Once again she was playing a historical figure, Morgaine, in the story of a battle with warriors from another dimension. *Battlefield* also saw the return of Bessie, which the Brigadier had apparently been keeping in store just in case the Doctor might ever have need of her again!

Ace, the Doctor's streetwise young companion, played by Sophie Aldred.

For Sophie Aldred, *The Curse of Fenric* by Ian Briggs provided some monsters even more scary than the Cybermen. This story of an ancient evil which threatened a World War Two naval base was filmed at Hawkhurst in Kent and the Crowborough Training Camp in East Sussex.

'The monsters were called Haemovores and they were after people's blood,' Sophie recalled later. 'According to the Doctor, Haemovore was the correct technical term, but they were vampires to me. They were really horrible with hideously deformed faces and they were supposed to be what human beings evolve into in millions of years' time.'

No one was aware while they were working on *Survival* that it would be the last story made solely by the BBC to be screened (*Ghost Light* was made later but screened earlier), although John Nathan-Turner had already indicated he was planning to move on once the last story was complete. Despite the fact that when the Rona Munro story began its three week run on 22 November 1989, it achieved the highest audience rating for the series – just over five million – the figures for the other stories which all had to compete against *Coronation Street* were as much as two million fewer. Just before Christmas, a statement from the BBC announced that there were no plans for a twenty-seventh series in the foreseeable future. It was made clear, too, that if *Doctor Who* was to return, then it would have to be made by an independent company. For Sylvester, who had signed to do three years as the Doctor with an option for a fourth season, it was a disappointing end to his tenure.

'I wasn't very pleased with the way it finished,' he says today without rancour. 'I just happened to be around when it was being mucked about with and there was nothing I could do other than my best. But I am a professional actor and you just have to say to yourself, "Well, I've been there, I've done that, and now I must get on with the next job." I'm a Leo which makes me a bit like a cat and that's very appropriate. I had a

Return of the Daleks in the 'explosive' story *Remembrance of the Daleks* filmed in London in April 1988.

childhood that feels as if it belonged to someone else. Then I worked in the City for a bit before becoming a hippy. Finally, I became an actor – four lives down and five to go!'

Unlike most of his predecessors, Sylvester did not find himself as weighed down by the role at the end. Initially, he did wonder if it might prove to be 'an albatross around my neck', but once the uncertainty about the programme's future had been resolved, he was free to get on with his career. There were some jobs he suspected he would not be considered for, but others which challenged his versatility would take their place. So it has proved.

Sylvester is today a popular guest at conventions, and enjoys referring to himself as 'another of the ex-Doctors'. He also appeared with Jon Pertwee, Tom Baker, Peter Davison and Colin Baker in the *Children in Need* skit *Dimensions in Time* in 1993, with Kate O'Mara as the Rani helping him to finish his career as he had begun it. However, he was not *quite* finished with *Doctor Who*. For just six years after he was last seen walking the familiar streets of London in *Survival*, Sylvester McCoy was asked to step one more time into the Doctor's shoes and pass the role on to another incumbent . . .

The Doctor and the Diddyman

The story of *Delta and the Bannermen* by Malcolm Kohl was set against the background of a holiday camp in the fifties and who better to have as the guest star than Ken Dodd, already a popular entertainer then and still probably the greatest comedian in the old musical hall tradition. By a piece of good fortune, the production team also found a location virtually unchanged from the era, the Majestic Holiday Camp at Barry Island in Wales. Once the cast and crew came on site in July 1987, the camp quickly became known as 'Who-de-Who', parodying the popular seaside comedy TV series, *Hi-De-Hi*.

Delta and the Bannermen was regarded by producer John Nathan-Turner as a 'fifties pastiche musical'. In it, the Doctor and Mel become involved with the Tollmaster – 'a cross between a game-show host and a pantomime dame', to quote Nathan-Turner – and the sinister Bannermen disguised as humans who crash-land their space-travelling coach into the 'Shangri-La' camp in Wales at the height of the holiday season. When the part of the Tollmaster was offered to Ken Dodd, he accepted it immediately – and even made a detour to Barry Island for a photocall prior to his own filming while on the way to a theatrical engagement in the north. He instantly captivated the waiting press corps as he posed for photographs with his co-stars. 'I'm tickled,' he told the journalists; '*Doctor Who* is one of the great British traditions like Test matches and pantos.'

In typical fashion, he described the character he was playing as 'a wild-eyed space nutter in a lilac silk suit with lots of spangles who guards a galactic toll-gate', and said he regarded the Tollmaster as a cross between David Bowie and Nigel Lawson (then the Chancellor of the Exchequer) 'because he wears fantastic clothes and he takes people's money off them'.

Ken Dodd's scenes in the story were all filmed during a night shoot, and members of the cast and crew all remember the arrival of the star in his car at the nearby Llandow Trading Estate where an old hangar had been designed to look like a toll-gate. The complete professional, Ken had already studied the script and turned up with all the props required for his scenes: a clip-board, party streamers, a razzer to play and so on. He informed Nathan-Turner he had brought them because he thought they would be too busy to sort them out and, anyway, he always travelled with a whole range of props in his car! The comic also amused the producer by constantly referring to him as 'Commander'.

During one scene when the Tollmaster was talking to a group of holidaymakers, all the actors were asked to ad lib. Ken Dodd immediately slipped into one of his familiar routines and so amused the entire set that director Chris Clough could hardly bring himself to shout 'Cut!' Ken also memorably addressed a plump husband who was accompanied by his equally large wife, 'Welcome, sir! I see you've brought your bulldog!'

Sylvester McCoy, who describes Ken Dodd as 'one of my gods', says the only sad thing about the shoot was the short time the star was on location. 'He was a very ordinary bloke until he had to do the performance. The remarkable thing was that with all his experience, he was still very concerned about playing the part because he hadn't done a lot of that type of acting. But he was wonderful.'

Ken Dodd's appearance in *Doctor Who* generated a considerable amount of publicity for *Delta and the Bannermen* when it was broadcast in November 1987 as well as good reviews and some amusing correspondence in *Radio Times*. 'Will there be a spin-off series?' Christopher Castleton of Cheltenham asked, 'Ken Dodd and his Diddymen against the Daleks?'

The Doctor Goes to Hollywood

? In the chilly winter days of January, it is difficult to mistake Vancouver, the vibrant city on Canada's Pacific coast, for anything other than what it is – the country's chief port and a major air and rail terminus which connects it to the rest of the country, as well as the USA just a few miles to the south. Yet this is the place which has become famous in movie-making terms as, firstly, where *The X-Files* series is made and, more recently, the location for the Doctor's 1996 adventure, *Doctor Who – The Movie* wherein the Canadian industrial city doubled successfully for San Francisco: the real thing almost a thousand miles away on the coast of California.

It was actually to an industrial estate on the outskirts of Vancouver that Paul McGann came in January 1996 to make the first new *Doctor Who* story in almost seven years. The filming was a testament not only to the enduring nature of the character himself, but also the perseverance of a number of people anxious to see the Time Lord on television once again.

The New Westminster estate is a mixture of factories and industrial buildings, many of them devoted in one way or another to the city's major industries which include engineering, textiles, paper, petroleum, even aeronautics and lumbering. One of the buildings bears the faded lettering of the Arkwright Hardware Company and, at first glance, seemed very little different to any of the others. On the outside, that is – because inside from 17 January 1996 for the next three months some of the most crucial scenes of *Doctor Who – The Movie* were filmed during the making of the $5 million, 90-minute special.

ACTOR: **Paul McGann (1959–)**

TIME-SPAN: **1996**

CHARACTERISTICS: **Handsome, debonair young Doctor who has to pit his wits – and several lifetimes of experience – against an old adversary, the Master. Supremely clever and adept at handling the latest Earth technology, he is also the first Time Lord to prove susceptible to the charms of a beautiful woman.**

APPEARANCE: **The most stylish dresser of all the Doctors in a matching outfit of various shades of brown. He wears a long, dark-brown frock coat with ornate buttons, and full cut light brown trousers. Beneath the jacket is a satin, patterned waistcoat and a silver watch chain. His wing-collared shirt marks a return to the style of the first Doctor and is worn with a large, light brown cravat. Like his great forebear, too, the latest regeneration wears a long wig – but of brown curls.**

In one corner of the vast, hangar-like Arkwright building stood the unmistakable and unobtrusive TARDIS completely overshadowed by the huge set of the Cloister room where the Doctor would once more confront his great foe, the Master, risen again as the personification of evil. Beyond this loomed a second, equally impressive set representing the TARDIS control room which had also been created out of plywood, paint, paper and electronic gadgetry by the wizardry of designer Richard Hudolin and his production team. Walking into the building for the first time on that January morning brought Paul McGann face to face with the reality of recreating a modern icon for the ninth time.

'At first, I could not imagine myself in the role – wearing that costume, saying those things, doing those things,' Paul has admitted. 'There are such expectations about the character among so many people. Although I had loved the Doctor on TV as a child it just did not seem like one of those things I could do. But then you have to be practical and weigh everything up. I am a parent, with bills and a mortgage to pay. And what I do is act. So I decided to take it.'

There seems no doubt that Paul McGann really *didn't* want to be the Doctor. But during a number of discussions with the executive producer, Philip Segal, a lifelong *Doctor Who* fan, Paul began to see how the part could be an interesting one for him. And because he is a friend of Sylvester McCoy he knew he would get lots of advice from his predecessor. Indeed, both men speak of each other with admiration and affection and the fact remains that probably no other regeneration in the series was effected with such good humour . . . nor quite so far away from where the legend had begun.

Paul, with his poetic-looking face, striking blue eyes and tongue-in-cheek patter delivered in a Liverpool twang, has come a long and not always easy route in his chosen profession. Badly treated by the press on a number of occasions – in particular over his private life – he can be distant and slightly intimidating when first met, but those who know him describe him as a warm and gregarious man. He lives in a comfortable house in Bristol with his wife, Annie, a former theatrical stage manager, and their two sons, Joe and Jake, and says of the city that it has 'the same energy as London on a smaller scale, and is a good mix of town and country'.

It is here that the real McGann with his cropped hair and unostentatious style of clothes can avoid being the focus of attention and feels freest

The huge set of the TARDIS control room for *Doctor Who – The Movie* in Vancouver.

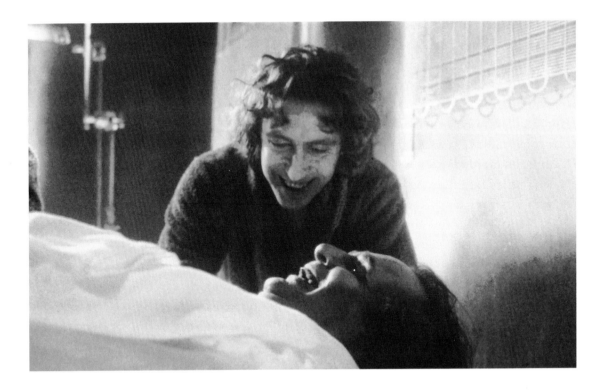

Paul McGann and Sylvester McCoy preparing to film the regeneration scene during the making of *Doctor Who – The Movie.*

to talk about his life and career. He enjoys working out at a local gym and most days when he is at home goes for a run on the Bristol Downs. 'It's beautiful there and I love the solitude,' he says, echoing the words of his predecessor, Pat Troughton, with whom he also shares a wicked sense of humour. To Paul, Doctor Who was a *job* – a one-off job as it turned out and one to which he brought the best of his talent and ability – and that is how he now likes to remember it.

Paul McGann was born on 14 November 1959, in Liverpool, the second of a family of four sons, Joe, Mark and Stephen, and a daughter, Clare. His father, Joe, was a metallurgist who worked for British Rail, and his mother, Clare, was a primary school teacher, until the untimely death of their father from heart disease in 1984. Paul remembers his childhood growing up in Birstall Road, Toxteth as 'ordinary' – though the fame as actors which has come to all four brothers has now caused the road to be re-named 'McGann Street' by local cabbies dropping fares in the vicinity.

The Catholic McGann family grew up in a terraced house not far from the docks with a kind of 'collective self-confidence' Paul says, although he describes himself as having been a private child. He was fascinated by the theatricalities of the Latin mass at church and believes this was partly responsible for the eventual career of himself and his brothers who all served as choir boys and altar boys.

'Look no further for our theatrical roots,' he told Jan Moir of the *Daily Telegraph.* 'It was the songs, the frocks, the incense, all the trappings. It was high and mighty and thrilling. When we get together now, we still like to sing Latin hymns in four-part harmony. Our mum loves it.'

Paul also appeared regularly in plays at the Cardinal Allen School which he attended with his brothers. There, one of the teachers planted the seed of his future life by telling him after a particularly impressive performance he had 'an indefinable something'. Yet Paul kept these tendencies to himself, explaining some years later: 'School was thick with assassins of the bogus. Anything highfalutin, any weaknesses were stamped on. If you harboured theatrical ambitions, you kept them to yourself.' Paul did just that and told anyone who asked he wanted to be a PE teacher – a not unlikely story as sport was one of his strong subjects and he played cricket for the Lancashire junior team as well as becoming Great Britain's triple jump champion when he was just 17.

At home, however, his mother and father encouraged all their children to follow their inclinations. 'They were wonderful parents,' he says. 'They pushed us to get O-levels and then told us to do whatever we wanted and be happy. I remember coming home after being out all night, and my mum knowing I was distressed about something. She'd say, "Where have you been?" and I wouldn't tell her. Then she'd ask if I was OK and I'd say, "Yes. No. I don't know." She'd use a kind of code to get us to talk.'

After leaving school with five O-levels and A-levels in Art and French, Paul worked briefly in an office before leaving for London. Here he intended to see if what the master at Cardinal Allen School had said was true – and enrolled at RADA where one of his contemporaries was Kenneth Branagh. After completing the course, Paul's early work was on the stage in productions as varied as the Beatles tributes, *John, Paul, George, Ringo . . . and Bert* and small classical roles in *Much Ado About Nothing* (where he met Annie) and *The Seagull*. In the interim Joe, Mark and Stephen had all become actors, too, and in 1985 they made showbusiness history when they became the first four brothers ever to co-star on the London stage in the West End musical, *Yackety Yak*. (In 1990, the continued success of all four inspired the *Daily Mirror* writer, Patricia Smyllie, to refer to them as 'The Magnificent McGanns – the most fabulous foursome to come out of Liverpool since the Beatles'.)

The Doctor uses a curiously archaic 'prop' during filming in Canada.

In 1983, Paul caught the eye of television viewers when he played the snooker whizz-kid Mo Morris in the BBC's *Give Us A Break* which co-starred Robert Lindsey as his seedy promoter. Two years later, he looked set to become the star of the HTV series, *Robin of Sherwood* when Michael Pared announced he was leaving to go to America and Paul was in the final line-up of actors. Instead the role went to Jason Connery. But out of this disappointment came the triumph of *The Monocled Mutineer* for the BBC which still remains one of his most acclaimed roles and one of which he is particularly proud. Written by Alan Bleasdale and allegedly based on real events, it told the strongly political story of a First World War soldier, Percy Toplis, who was involved in a mass mutiny of troops in 1917 and as a result hunted down by the military authorities and shot *two years* after the end of the hostilities. The controversy in the press and on television about the 'truth' of the story only enhanced his reputation.

Paul made his feature film debut in 1987 in *Withnail and I*, co-starring with Richard E. Grant in the story of two 'resting' actors fresh from drama school who are heavily into drugs, drink and music. Paul played the 'I' of the title in this groundbreaking movie which has since been compared to *Trainspotting*. Of his character, he has said: 'He's the man with no name, but nothing ever happens in the story without him being there. There's a lot of me in the character. I had a similar kind of relationship at drama school – a sort of fascination with someone you know is burning out.'

An actor with less determination than Paul might indeed have burned himself out when, as a result of the success of the low-budget movie, he was hired to work in Hollywood. Unhappily, much of his work on Steven Spielberg's *Empire of the Sun* ended on the cutting room floor, and he fared little better in *Alien 3* when his part ultimately lasted for no more than three minutes on screen. Things got no better on his return to London, for in September 1992 he was flown out to the Crimea to begin filming in Central TV's historical series about the resourceful soldier, *Sharpe*, based on the novels by Bernard Cornwell. After only a few days of filming, he damaged a knee while playing a game of football with the crew and actors and had to be flown home. His part was taken by Sean Bean and the rest, of course, is history.

Not surprisingly, Paul remembers this part of his career very clearly. 'I whinged like a bastard for seven months,' he said later. 'I had never been injured before, and it really knocked my confidence – and this game is all about confidence. What made it worse was I was only doing *Sharpe* for the money, because I was skint. And it was *fantastic* money.'

For the first time in his life, Paul says, he found himself being really tested. He had always regarded himself as someone who breezed through life and the injury suddenly made him worry about the future. All the more so because he was a parent. It was the surgeon who operated on his leg who all unknowingly gave him a boost when he said the next part he landed would probably be in an all-action production, perhaps even a swashbuckler. When his agent rang him to tell him he had been offered a part in *The Three Musketeers*, he could hardly stop smiling for days.

The year 1995 saw Paul reunited with his three brothers in a film for BBC Northern Ireland about the Irish potato famine. The idea for *The Hanging Gale* had actually occurred to Stephen McGann while he was investigating the family's history in Ireland and came across the story of an ancestor named Eugene McGann who had become a refugee from the famine. The four-part saga which was largely filmed on location in Donegal described the struggles of a family to survive during those terrible times and once again demonstrated the versatility of the McGann family in their ensemble performances.

At the time Paul was filming *The Hanging Gale* word was already going around the acting profession that a new *Doctor Who* series was being contemplated. Although he was not aware of the facts at the time, a number of film makers had been trying for some time to get permission from the BBC to bring the Doctor back to the screen as soon as the Corporation had announced that the future for *Doctor Who* lay in having it made independently. To a man (and woman) these groups had all formerly been involved with the programme.

At the forefront was Verity Lambert who had never lost her interest in the show and now had her own company, Cinema Verity. There were also the Dalek and Cybermen creators, Terry Nation and Gerry Davis, who claimed to have the support of the Walt Disney Corporation for a twenty-episode series; and a former scriptwriter on the series, Victor Pemberton, whose Saffron Productions had Hollywood interest, too. Three former *Doctor Who* special effects experts, George Dugdale, John Humphreys and Peter Litten, similarly put forward plans to make a big-budget movie and formed a consortium with a number of showbusiness stars including Bryan Ferry and John Isley of Dire Straits. This group, too, claimed to have interested Warner Brothers, and were said to have even got as far as considering the likes of Bill Cosby, Denholm Elliott, Donald Sutherland and Alan Rickman as a possible new Doctor! For the main villain the trio and their American backers were said to favour Jack Nicholson.

As it transpired, it was a *fan* of the series, Philip Segal – once a resident of Southend in Essex who had watched the show from its inception with his grandfather and now a senior television executive in Hollywood – who finally secured the BBC's permission to make the long-awaited new movie under the umbrella of Universal Pictures. He came to the project with two successful sf productions behind him, *SeaQuest DSV* – inspired by Jules Verne's novel *Voyage to the Bottom of the Sea* – and *Earth 2*. Getting *Doctor Who* made, however, also owed a lot to the support of another Englishman, Trevor Walton, a vice-president at Fox TV in the USA who agreed to co-finance the deal, and Jo Wright, the executive producer at the BBC. With agreement reached between the three parties in 1995, Philip Segal then persuaded Paul McGann to become the new Doctor.

The press had a field day while all this behind the scenes activity was going on – especially in suggesting the names of stars who might be up for the leading role. Among those who were tipped was the former *Monty Python* star, Eric Idle (with *Baywatch*'s Pamela Anderson as his companion!), Dudley Moore, John Cleese, the singer, Sting, and even David Hasselhoff as 'a street-wise American Time Lord'. And if not any of them, then the *Sunday Mirror* reported that the Doctor might just change sex – as Tom Baker had once suggested – and be played by the British actress, Carolyn Seymour.

But Philip Segal had no such intentions as he insisted in an interview with *The Times* while production of the film was in progress. 'The Doctor is a very special character,' he said. 'Kids don't have enough heroes and he is a hero in every sense of the word. He is not this square-jawed handsome guy; he is every person's hero. As a boy, I was not in a clique. I did not have a lot of friends. He was the guy who was saying, "It's OK to be different, it's OK to be you".'

Part of Philip's deal with the BBC was to ensure the actor who played the Doctor was British and that the figure was not to be embarrassed in any way. 'I am doing this because I am a fan and I want the series back as much as everybody else. I'm not interested in tearing the fabric of the show apart. These are the icons. If you are not going to buy into the icons people associate with the series, then don't do it.

'Ultimately, of course, the Doctor *is* an alien,' he added. 'He's not from England – he's from another planet. We set out to create an international *Doctor Who*.'

For Paul to agree to Segal's overtures seemed somehow fated. For didn't McGann come from Liverpool like Tom Baker and weren't they both the same age when introduced in the role? Paul also liked the fact that apart from Segal and Walton who were both English, the director, Geoffrey Sax and scriptwriter Matthew Jacobs came from Britain, too. Sax had, in fact, already worked for the BBC drama department on series such as *Bergerac* and *Lovejoy* and was familiar with the demands of a long-running tradition; while Matthew Jacobs could claim an actor father, Anthony Jacobs, who had actually appeared in one of the first Doctor's stories, *The Gunfighters*, as Doc Holliday. Matthew was just six years old when his father took him to the set to meet William Hartnell and this, he says, sparked a life-long interest in the series which culminated in being asked by Segal to write the script for the latest reincarnation. The writer and star soon found they shared something else in common.

'Tom Baker was brilliant as the Doctor, but William Hartnell was certainly the governor even if he was a cantankerous sod!' Paul said during a press visit to the set in Vancouver while shooting was taking place. 'I used to watch the series when I was a kid and Bill Hartnell used to terrify me. He was himself, literally; a Victorian with something stern and old-fashioned about him. When you talk about the villains, my favourite was the Yeti. The Daleks never did it for me – they couldn't climb upstairs.'

Once he had agreed to play the latest regeneration of the Doctor, Paul knew he had to play it *his* way. 'I looked for something more edgy than the others,' he said. 'It's like the vampire. You can't have hung round for three hundred years and not feel kind of bitter. So there were darker elements to my Doctor.'

Paul fully expected comparisons to be made with the earlier incarnations, but was determined to create a character full of interest for him – and one who would continue to challenge his skills *if* the plans for a further six, fifty-minute episodes materialised. Even as the work went on, outlines were already being discussed for the Doctor to confront the Daleks again on Skaro; to defeat the Cybermen in another attempt to conquer Earth; and even to go *back* in time to the era of Napoleon.

Another factor that made filming enjoyable for Paul was having Sylvester McCoy along for part of the time. 'He was the first person on the phone when I got the role, giving me the low-down,' Paul says. 'He told me everything I needed to know. He also told me, "You can't win and you can't lose. Some people will hate you and others will love you." It's as simple as that.'

Sylvester, for his part, was happy to pass on the role and regarded the trip to Vancouver as something of a golden handshake. He admitted to having reservations when first hearing his friend had landed the role – feeling the production team had opted to go for a younger doctor again because of the 'cult of youth' – but revised his view when he saw Paul's steely, almost dangerous quality combined with a certain humorous element at work.

Shooting the change-over of the Doctors was, however, a long process and involved a total of nine days' filming. McCoy's Doctor was seen arriving in the TARDIS in San Francisco on the eve of the Millennium only to be gunned down by a street gang. Then when the eminent cardiologist Dr Grace Holloway (Daphne Ashbrook) attempts to save his life, she is unaware the Doctor has two hearts and kills off McCoy, thereby

Daphne Ashbrook, as Dr Grace Holloway, was the first of the Doctor's companions ever to kiss the Time Lord.

allowing McGann to metamorphose in his place. Bewildered at who he is – and *where* he is – the new Doctor turns to Grace for help; help that is all the more valuable when the Master (Eric Roberts) reappears in San Francisco up to all his old machinations.

Like Daphne Ashbrook, the small and wiry Roberts, forever described as Julia Roberts' brother, had been cast because he was American, a 'name' on television and was felt to have the necessary gravitas to bring in new viewers to *Doctor Who*. Interestingly, he had actually seen the series on TV in 1973 while he was studying at RADA. 'We all sat around watching this programme saying how awfully cheesy it was – but no one would turn it off,' he has recalled. 'Playing this part which has also been done by two other guys was also great.'

Paul McGann actually filmed some of his very first scenes as the Doctor with Daphne Ashbrook. The Los Angeles-born actress, well-known in *Falcon Crest*, admitted she had never heard of *Doctor Who* before being cast and her only previous work on a sf series had been in *Star Trek: Deep Space Nine* in which she played a wheelchair-bound character, Merlora. These scenes had involved hours in make-up which she found infinitely less satisfying than playing Grace Holloway which, she said, allowed her lively, intelligent personality full rein.

'I really had no idea that *Doctor Who* had such a fanatical following,' she also said during filming. 'It wasn't until I heard Sylvester McCoy telling Paul that he had no idea what he was taking on that I realised. But there was no way I was going to be another of the Doctor's helpless companions. Grace is a nineties woman, very strong-willed, who does her own thing. Certainly she finds the Doctor attractive, but their relationship is an equal one in many ways.'

Working on the scenes with Daphne while he was struggling to discover his identity helped Paul to 'find' the Doctor he wanted to play – that and wearing his costume and, especially, putting on his *shoes*. Like a number of actors who pay great attention to getting themselves *into* a role, Paul believes in the old adage that clothes can make a character. In his case, the story required him to select an outfit from a locker full of party clothes after he has regenerated and finds himself wearing nothing other than a hospital shroud.

'On the first day, you just think of yourself as the latest bloke to wear the outfit,' he explains, 'which can be a bit intimidating especially if you think of some of the actors who have played the Doctor before like

Hartnell, Troughton and the others. But because I wasn't up on all the intricacies, I decided the best thing was just to get on the set and *do* it. Geoffrey Sax was great and obviously understood the character and helped me to make it work.'

One element of *Doctor Who – The Movie* which moved into new territory was the romantic frisson between the Doctor and Grace Holloway. Paul McGann, for his part, was unaware that the Time Lord had never kissed a woman on screen before, though there had been suggestions that Tom Baker's Doctor had a romantic element somewhere in his character. Paul was, though, determined that no sexual innuendo would creep into the Doctor's first kiss; all the more so after discussing the matter with his agent, Janet Fielding, who had herself, of course, been one of Peter Davison's companions, Tegan. According to a story Paul tells with relish, Janet's unflattering assessment of that side of the Doctor's character was, 'Two hearts, no dick!' As a result, he responded to rumours in the tabloids that Doctor Who was about to 'get his leg over' his latest companion, in a manner that left no room for misunderstanding.

Paul McGann in the climactic fight sequence with the latest reincarnation of the Master, Eric Roberts.

'I kept my lips closed during the kiss – I felt I had to,' he said. 'The Doctor has just discovered who he is and is so pleased that he gives Grace a kiss almost without thinking about it. The director was on a long lens at the time so they didn't notice it until it was too late. I know it is over thirty years down the line, but the Doctor has always been a very *childlike* character. If they had asked me to do a bedroom scene I would have said no. What would be the point?'

Paul remains objective about his work on the film and, despite the assurance in his performance, felt that for much of the time he was 'just hanging on' in the role. He did, though, enjoy the working atmosphere and sheer professionalism of those in the production team who, he believes, were all aware of the tradition they were upholding. The storyline might well not have been as deep on the mythology of the Doctor Who legend as its predecessors, but certainly fulfilled Philip Segal's intention of making the Time Lord more of an international figure.

What worried Paul far more than playing the part was the thought of attending fan conventions. An intensely private person who says he is shy in front of large numbers of people, he has so far resisted all invitations to speak. He did discuss the subject with Sylvester McCoy and seriously considered one of his predecessor's ideas. McCoy suggested that as Paul looked so different out of his flowing, curly wig and frock coat, he might turn up at a gathering in an anorak and just mingle among the fans to see for himself!

'But the idea of going to a convention just fills me with absolute dread,' he says, honestly. 'I know it's something I'll do one day, just to scare myself and prove to myself that I can do it. But I'm nervous by nature and it will take a lot of will power. That's also the reason why I'm happier doing films and television rather than theatre.'

Paul also still smiles over Sylvester McCoy's comparison of him to the most short-lived of the James Bond actors – 'the George Lazenby of Time Lords'. But even though the option clause in his contract to play the Doctor has now run out and it is unlikely he would return if offered the chance, Paul McGann remains convinced that the series is not dead. He believes the concept is as valid now as when it was devised thirty-five years ago by Sydney Newman.

'I enjoyed playing the Doctor,' he says, choosing his final words carefully. 'I had a go and things didn't work out. But I'm sure somebody else will have a crack one day. After all, he has got thirteen lives, hasn't he?'

That Doctor Is a Lady!

After all the years of hints and suggestions, the Doctor finally *did* regenerate into a woman in the 'Comic Relief' special, *The Curse of the Fatal Death*, televised on 12 March 1999. The four-part story also saw the Time Lord adopt four new male personalities, taking the tally to an ominous 13. What's more, the Doctor even suggested he was thinking of 'retiring and getting married'!

The decision to bring the Doctor back to the BBC television studios for the first time in nearly ten years was that of producer, Sue Vertue, and 'Comic Relief' mastermind, Richard Curtis, co-creator of *Blackadder*, who cast its star, Rowan Atkinson, as the 'unofficial' ninth television Time Lord. The script of *The Curse of the Fatal Death* was by Steven Moffat, who transported the Doctor and his latest companion, Emma (Julia Sawalha), to the planet Tersurus and a confrontation with the Master, played by Jonathan Pryce. A bizarre battle of wits between the two was brought to an abrupt end by the arrival of the Daleks who imprisoned the Doctor and Emma in a mountaintop citadel. However, by using guile, wit and the odd gaseous eruption, the Doctor managed to escape: although during an exchange of gunfire he was shot and once more began to regenerate. This time, though, there were three false starts before the 'new' Doctor – now female – left Tersurus, arm in arm with the Master . . .

Directed by John Henderson, the 20-minute special was the most lavish parody of *Doctor Who* ever produced, complete with a very impressive cast list, special effects and five new Daleks with state-of-the-art weaponry. A highlight among the many comic moments was the sight of the Master's TARDIS console, which had been deliberately built to wobble in homage to the show's reputation (actually undeserved) for rickety sets. Fans were also provided with a tenuous explanation as to the Master's fate between *Frontier in Space* and *The Deadly Assassin* when his repeated dumping into pits of raw sewage caused him to become steadily more aged and decrepit.

The actors who played the post-Atkinson regenerations were Richard E. Grant (who had, of course, co-starred with Paul McGann in *Withnail and I*), Jim Broadbent from *The Avengers*, and Hugh Grant, star of *Four Weddings and a Funeral*. It was left to Joanna Lumley – tipped from the mid-eighties as an ideal choice if the Doctor became a female – to steal the show as the final reincarnation of the Time Lord.

Doctor Who Preservation Archive

This archive has been compiled by Jeremy Bentham, one of the most knowledgeable authorities on the saga of *Doctor Who*. Herein he provides details of all the media in which the various adventures of the Doctor are available, whether on film, video or books, thereby enabling any reader to enjoy the original story in one form or another. The BBC are, of course, continuing to release videos from the series and they remain optimistic that more 'missing' episodes of the kind which have been rediscovered in recent years in the most unexpected places all over the world will continue to come to light in the future.

Abbreviations:
B&W – Black and White
DWM – Doctor Who Magazine (Marvel Comics)
DWCC – Doctor Who Classic Comic (Marvel Comics)
DWB – Dream Watch Bulletin
VT – video tape

Story title Writers *UK premiered*	Surviving episodes Media	BBC video released	Novel title Author *First published*	Other media

1963

| **An Unearthly Child/100,000 BC**
(aka The Tribe of Gum)
Anthony Coburn (C.E. Webber)
23 November | 1–4 (All)
16mm B&W film & pilot
episode
(two versions) | **April 1990** Ep. 4 edited
June 1991 Pilot on *The Hartnell Years* VT | **Same as TV title**
Terrance Dicks
October 1981 | **Script Book**
(Titan Jan 1988) |
| **The Daleks**
(aka The Mutants)
Terry Nation
21 December | 1–7
16mm B&W film | **June 1989** Ep. 7 edited 2 cassettes | **Same as TV title**
David Whitaker
September 1964 | **Telesnaps**
D W Annual 1964

Script Book
(Titan Dec 1989)

Filmed as *Dr Who and the Daleks* |

1964

Inside the Spaceship *(aka Edge of Destruction/Beyond the Sun)* David Whitaker *8 February*	1–2 (All) 16mm B&W film		**The Edge of Destruction** Nigel Robinson *May 1988*	
Marco Polo *(aka The Journey to Cathay)* John Lucarotti *22 February*	**None**		**Same as TV title** John Lucarotti *December 1984*	
The Keys of Marinus Terry Nation *11 March*	1-6 (All) 16mm B&W film	**March 1999**	**Same as TV title** Philip Hinchcliffe *August 1980*	
The Aztecs John Lucarotti *23 April*	1-4 (All) 16mm B&W film	**November 1992**	**Same as TV title** John Lucarotti *June 1984*	
The Sensorites Peter R. Newman *20 May*	1–6 (All) 16mm B&W film		**Same as TV title** Nigel Robinson *February 1987*	
The Reign of Terror Dennis Spooner *8 July*	1–3, 6 16mm B&W film (& some amateur clips footage)		**Same as TV title** Ian Marter *March 1987*	
Planet of Giants Louis Marks *31 October*	1–3 (All) 16mm B&W film		**Same as TV title** Terrance Dicks *January 1990*	
The Dalek Invasion of Earth Terry Nation *21 November*	1–6 (All) 16mm B&W film & ep. 5 35mm telerecording	**May 1990** 2 cassettes	**Same as TV title** Terrance Dicks *March 1977*	**Filmed as** *The Daleks: Invasion Earth 2150 AD*

1965

| **The Rescue**
David Whitaker
2 January | 1–2 (All)
16mm B&W film | **September 1994**
2 cassettes with *The Romans* | **Same as TV title**
Ian Marter
August 1987 | |
| **The Romans**
Dennis Spooner
16 January | 1–4 (All)
16mm B&W film | **September 1994**
2 cassettes with *The Rescue* | **Same as TV title**
Donald Cotton
April 1987 | |

Story title Writers *UK premiered*	Surviving episodes Media	BBC video released	Novel title Author *First published*	Other media
The Web Planet Bill Strutton *13 February*	**1–6 (All)** 16mm B&W film	**September 1990** 2 cassettes, eps & 6 edited	**The Zarbi** Bill Strutton *September 1965*	
The Crusade David Whitaker *22 March*	**1, 3** 16mm B&W film	**June 1991** as part of *The Hartnell Years* VT (ep. 3 only) **June 1999** with *The Space Museum*	**The Crusaders** David Whitaker *September 1965*	**Script Book** (Titan Nov 1994)
The Space Museum Glyn Jones *24 April*	**1–4 (All)** 16mm B&W film	**June 1999** with *The Crusade* (eps. 1 & 3 only)	**Same as TV title** Glyn Jones *January 1987*	
The Chase Terry Nation *22 May*	**1–6 (All)** 16mm B&W film	**September 1993** in 30th anniversary commemorative tin & booklet	**Same as TV title** John Peel *July 1989*	**Audio** THE DALEKS – abridged ep. 6 soundtrack, Century 21 EP 1965
Film: Dr Who and the Daleks Milton Subotsky (Terry Nation) *25 June*	35mm colour Panavision (Techniscope) film	**1982** (pan & scan version) Thorn/EMI **1993** (widescreen version) Lumiere		**DELL comic book 1966** **Photo-story in Dalek Annual 1965**
The Time Meddler Dennis Spooner *3 July*	**1–4 (All)** 16mm B&W film		**Same as TV title** Nigel Robinson *October 1987*	
Galaxy Four William Emms *11 September*	**None** (some 16mm clips footage)		**Same as TV title** William Emms *November 1985*	**Script Book** (Titan Jul 1994)
Mission to the Unknown *(aka Dalek Cutaway)* Terry Nation *9 October*	**None**		**The Daleks' Master Plan I** John Peel *September 1989*	
The Myth Makers Donald Cotton *16 October*	**None** (some amateur clips footage)		**Same as TV title** Donald Cotton *April 1985*	
The Daleks' Master Plan Terry Nation & Dennis Spooner *13 November*	**5, 10** 16mm B&W film (& some clips footage)	**July 1992** as part of *Daleks – The Early Years* VT	**The Daleks' Master Plan I & II** John Peel *September/October 1989*	

1966

The Massacre of St Bartholomew's Eve John Lucarotti & Donald Tosh *5 February*	**None**		**The Massacre** John Lucarotti *June 1987*	
The Ark Paul Erickson & Lesley Scott *5 March*	**1–4 (All)** 16mm B&W film	**October 1998**	**Same as TV title** Paul Erickson *October 1986*	
The Celestial Toymaker Brian Hayles, Gerry Davis, John Wiles & Donald Tosh *2 April*	**3** 16mm B&W film	**June 1991** as part of *The Hartnell Years* VT	**Same as TV title** Gerry Davis/Alison Bingeman *June 1986*	
The Gunfighters Donald Cotton *30 April*	**1–4 (All)** 16mm B&W film		**Same as TV title** Donald Cotton *July 1985*	**Telesnaps** exist

Story title Writers *UK premiered*	Surviving episodes Media	BBC video released	Novel title Author *First published*	Other media
The Savages Ian Stuart Black *28 May*	**None** (some amateur clips footage)		Same as TV title Ian Stuart Black *March 1986*	**Telesnaps** exist
The War Machines Ian Stuart Black & Kit Pedler *25 June*	**1–4 (All)** 16mm B&W film	**June 1997** restored re-edited	Same as TV title Ian Stuart Black *February 1989*	**Telesnaps** exist
The Smugglers Brian Hayles *9 September*	**None** (some 16mm & amateur clips footage)		Same as TV title Terrance Dicks *June 1988*	**Telesnaps** DWM 217
The Tenth Planet Kit Pedler & Gerry Davis *8 October*	**1–3** 16mm B&W film (some 16mm & amateur clips footage)		Same as TV title Gerry Davis *February 1976*	**Telesnaps** exist DWM 207 (ep. 4 only)
The Power of the Daleks David Whitaker & Dennis Spooner *5 November*	**None** (some 16mm & amateur clips footage)		Same as TV title John Peel *July 1993*	**Telesnaps** DWB Compendium 1993 **Audio** BBC Audio Collection Aug 93 **Script Book** (Titan Mar 1993)
The Highlanders Elwyn Jones & Gerry Davis *17 December*	**None** (some 16mm clips footage)		Same as TV title Gerry Davis *August 1984*	**Telesnaps** DWM 233–236
Film: Daleks – Invasion Earth 2150 AD Milton Subotsky/David Whitaker (Terry Nation) *5 August*	**35mm colour Panavision (Techniscope) film**	**1982** (pan & scan version) Thorn/EMI **1993** (Widescreen version) Lumiere	Same as TV title William Emms *November 1985*	**Script Book** (Titan Jul 1994)

1967

Story title	Surviving episodes	BBC video released	Novel title	Other media
The Underwater Menace Geoffrey Orme *14 January*	**3** 16mm B&W film (& some 16mm clips footage)	**November 1998** as part of *The Ice Warriors*	Same as TV title Nigel Robinson *February 1988*	**Telesnaps** DWM 233–236
The Moonbase Kit Pedler & Gerry Davis *11 February*	**2, 4** 16mm B&W film	**July 1992** as part of *Cybermen – The Early Years* VT	**The Cybermen** Gerry Davis *February 1975*	**Telesnaps** DWB Compendium 1993
The Macra Terror Ian Stuart Black *11 March*	**None** (some 16mm & amateur clips footage)		Same as TV title Ian Stuart Black *July 1987*	**Telesnaps** DWM 251–254 **Audio** BBC Audio Collection Jul 92
The Faceless Ones Davis Ellis & Malcolm Hulke *8 April*	**1, 3** 16mm B&W film		Same as TV title Terrance Dicks *December 1986*	**Telesnaps** DWM 260–265
The Evil of the Daleks David Whitaker *20 May*	**2** (& some 16mm clips footage)	**July 1992** as part of *Daleks – The Early Years* VT	Same as TV title John Peel *August 1993*	**Telesnaps** DWM 237–243 **Audio** BBC Audio Collection Jul 93

Story title Writers *UK premiered*	Surviving episodes Media	BBC video released	Novel title Author *First published*	Other media
The Tomb of the Cybermen Kit Pedler & Gerry Davis *2 September*	1–4 (All) 16mm B&W film	May 1992	Same as TV title Gerry Davis *May 1978*	**Telesnaps** exist **Audio** BBC Audio Collection Jul 93 CD of incidental music 1996 **Script Book** (Titan Aug 89)
The Abominable Snowmen Mervyn Haisman & Henry Lincoln *30 September*	2 16mm B&W film (& some 16mm clips footage)	June 1991 as part of *The Troughton Years* VT	Same as TV title Terrance Dicks *November 1974*	**Telesnaps** DWM 224–229
The Ice Warriors Brian Hayles *11 November*	1, 4–6 16mm B&W film	November 1998 4 episodes, CD & documentary	Same as TV title Brian Hayles *March 1976*	**Telesnaps** DWM 217–219 DWCC 24–26
The Enemy of the World David Whitaker & Derrick Sherwin *23 December*	3 16mm B&W film	June 1991 as part of *The Troughton Years* VT	Same as TV title Ian Marter *March 1981*	**Telesnaps** DWM 273–277 (no ep. 4)

1968

Story title	Surviving episodes	BBC video released	Novel title	Other media
The Web of Fear Mervyn Haisman & Henry Lincoln *3 February*	1 16mm B&W film		Same as TV title Terrance Dicks *August 1976*	**Telesnaps** DWM 211–213 DWCC 18–20
Fury from the Deep Victor Pemberton & Derrick Sherwin *16 March*	None (some 16mm & amateur clips footage)		Same as TV title Victor Pemberton *May 1986*	**Telesnaps** DWM 208–210 DWCC 15–17 **Audio** BBC Audio Collection Apr 93
The Wheel in Space David Whitaker & Kit Pedler *27 April*	3, 6 16mm & 35mm B&W film	July 1992 as part of *Cybermen – The Early Years* VT	Same as TV title Terrance Dicks *March 1988*	**Telesnaps** DWM 214–216 DWCC 21–23
The Dominators Norman Ashby (Mervyn Haisman & Henry Lincoln) *10 August*	1–5 (All) 16mm B&W film (& ep. 3 35mm telerecording)	September 1990	Same as TV title Ian Marter *April 1984*	**Telesnaps** exist except for 1 episode
The Mind Robber Peter Ling & Derrick Sherwin *14 September*	1–5 (All) 16mm B&W film (& ep. 5 35mm telerecording)	May 1990	Same as TV title Peter Ling *November 1986*	**Telesnaps** exist except for ep. 5
The Invasion Derrick Sherwin & Kit Pedler *2 November*	2, 3, 5–8 16mm B&W film	June 1993 episodes & links by Nicholas Courtney	Same as TV title Ian Marter *May 1985*	
The Krotons Robert Holmes *28 December*	1–4 (All) 16mm B&W film (& ep. 1 35mm telerecording)	February 1991	Same as TV title Terrance Dicks *June 1985*	

1969

Story title	Surviving episodes	BBC video released	Novel title	Other media
The Seeds of Death Brian Hayles and Terrance Dicks *25 January*	1–6 (All) 16mm B&W film	July 1985 omnibus	Same as TV title Terrance Dicks *July 1986*	

Story title Writers *UK premiered*	Surviving episodes Media	BBC video released	Novel title Author *First published*	Other media
The Space Pirates Robert Holmes *8 March*	2 (35mm telerecording)	**June 1991** as part of *The Troughton Years* VT	**Same as TV title** Terrance Dicks *March 1990*	
The War Games Terrance Dicks & Malcolm Hulke *19 April*	1–10 (All) 16mm B&W film	**February 1990** 2 cassettes	**Same as TV title** Malcolm Hulke *September 1979*	

1970

Spearhead from Space Robert Holmes *3 January*	1–4 (All) 16mm colour film	**February 1988** omnibus **February 1995**	**The Auton Invasion** Terrance Dicks *January 1974*	
Doctor Who and the Silurians Malcolm Hulke *31 January*	1–7 (All) 625-line PAL VT recoloured	**July 1993** full colourised version	**The Cave Monsters** Malcolm Hulke *January 1974*	
The Ambassadors of Death David Whitaker, Malcolm Hulke & Trevor Ray *21 March*	1–7 (All) 16mm B&W film (& ep. 1 625-line PAL 2" VT colour, ep. 5 625-line PAL VT recoloured)		**Same as TV title** Terrance Dicks *May 1987*	
Inferno Don Houghton *9 May*	1–7 (All) 525-line VT colour	**March 1992** ep. 7 on *The Pertwee Years* VT **April 1994** 2 cassettes	**Same as TV title** Terrance Dicks *July 1984*	**Audio** Incidental music available on compilation CD

1971

Terror of the Autons Robert Holmes *2 January*	1–4 (All) 625-line PAL VT recoloured	**April 1993** full colourised version	**Same as TV title** Terrance Dicks *April 1975*	
The Mind of Evil Don Houghton *30 January*	1–6 (All) 16mm B&W film (& some colour ep. 6 footage)	**May 1998** 2 cassettes B&W	**Same as TV title** Terrance Dicks *March 1985*	**Audio** Incidental music available on compilation CD
The Claws of Axos Bob Baker & Dave Martin *13 March*	1–4 (All) 1, 4 625-line PAL 2" VT colour 2, 3 525-line VT colour	**May 1992**	**Same as TV title** Terrance Dicks *April 1977*	
Colony in Space Malcolm Hulke *10 April*	1–6 (All) 525-line VT colour		**The Doomsday Weapon** Malcolm Hulke *March 1974*	
The Daemons Guy Leopold (Barry Letts & Robert Sloman) *22 May*	1–5 (All) 625-line PAL VT recoloured, ep. 4 625-line PAL 2" VT colour	**March 1992** ep. 5 on *The Pertwee Years* VT **February 1993** full colourised version	**Same as TV title** Barry Letts *May 1974*	**Script Book** (Titan Oct 1992)

1972

Day of the Daleks Louis Marks *1 January*	1–4 (All) 625-line PAL 2" VT colour	**July 1986** omnibus **January 1994**	**Same as TV title** Terrance Dicks *March 1974*	**Laser disc released** 1986, 1997
The Curse of Peladon Brian Hayles *29 January*	1–4 (All) 525-line VT colour	**August 1993**	**Same as TV title** Brian Hayles *November 1974*	**Audio** BBC Talking Book 1996

Story title Writers *UK premiered*	Surviving episodes Media	BBC video released	Novel title Author *First published*	Other media
The Sea Devils Malcolm Hulke *26 February*	1–6 (All) eps. 1–3 525-line VT colour eps. 4–6 625-line PAL 2" VT colour	September 1995 2 cassettes	**Same as TV title** Malcolm Hulke *June 1974*	**Audio** Incidental music available on compilation CD
The Mutants Bob Baker & Dave Martin *8 April*	1–6 (All) eps. 1–2 525-line VT colour eps. 3–6 625-line PAL 2" VT colour		**Same as TV title** Terrance Dicks *September 1977*	
The Time Monster Robert Sloman *20 May*	1–6 (All) 525-line VT colour (ep. 6 recolourised)		**Same as TV title** Terrance Dicks *September 1985*	
The Three Doctors Bob Baker & Dave Martin & Terrance Dicks *30 December*	1–4 (All) 625-line PAL 2" VT colour	August 1991	**Same as TV title** Terrance Dicks *November 1975*	

1973

Carnival of Monsters Robert Holmes *27 January*	1–4 (All) 625-line PAL 2" VT colour	March 1995	**Same as TV title** Terrance Dicks *January 1977*	
Frontier in Space Malcolm Hulke *24 February*	1–6 (All) 625-line PAL 2" VT colour	March 1992 ep. 6 on *The Pertwee Years* VT August 1995 2 cassettes	**The Space War** Malcolm Hulke *September 1976*	
Planet of the Daleks Terry Nation *7 April*	1–6 (All) 625-line PAL 2" VT colour except ep. 3 B&W 16mm film		**Same as TV title** Terrance Dicks *October 1976*	**Audio** BBC Talking Book 1996
The Green Death Robert Sloman *19 May*	1–6 (All) 625-line PAL 2" VT colour	November 1996 2 cassettes	**Same as TV title** Malcolm Hulke *August 1975*	
The Time Warrior Robert Holmes *15 December*	1–4 (All) 625-line PAL 2" VT colour	September 1989 omnibus October 1999	**Same as TV title** Terrance Dicks/Robert Holmes *June 1978*	

1974

Invasion of the Dinosaurs (aka *Invasion* – ep. 1 only) Malcolm Hulke *12 January*	1–6 (All) 625-line PAL 2" VT colour except ep. 1 B&W 16mm film	September 1999	**The Dinosaur Invasion** Malcolm Hulke *February 1976*	
Death to the Daleks Terry Nation *23 February*	1–4 (All) 625-line PAL 2" VT colour	October 1987 omnibus February 1995	**Same as TV title** Terrance Dicks *July 1978*	
The Monster of Peladon Brian Hayles *23 March*	1–6 (All) 625-line PAL 2" VT colour	January 1996 2 cassettes	**Same as TV title** Terrance Dicks *December 1980*	
Planet of the Spiders Robert Sloman *4 May*	1–6 (All) 625-line PAL 2" VT colour	April 1991 2 cassettes	**Same as TV title** Terrance Dicks *October 1975*	
Robot Terrance Dicks *28 December*	1–4 (All) 625-line PAL 2" VT colour	January 1992	**The Giant Robot** Terrance Dicks *March 1975*	

Story title Writers *UK premiered*	Surviving episodes Media	BBC video released	Novel title Author *First published*	Other media
1975				
The Ark in Space Robert Holmes & John Lucarotti *25 January*	1–4 (All) 625-line PAL 2" VT colour	**June 1989** omnibus **January 1994**	Same as TV title Ian Marter *May 1977*	**Laser disc pressing 1996** Incidental music available on compilation CD
The Sontaran Experiment Bob Baker & Dave Martin *22 February*	1–2 (All) 625-line PAL 2" VT colour	**October 1991** 2 cassettes, with *Genesis of the Daleks*	Same as TV title Ian Marter *December 1978*	
Genesis of the Daleks Terry Nation & Robert Holmes *8 March*	1–6 (All) 625-line PAL 2" VT colour	**October 1991** 2 cassettes, with *The Sontaran Experiment*	Same as TV title Terrance Dicks *July 1976*	**Audio** abridged BBC album 1979 Incidental music available on compilation CD
Revenge of the Cybermen Gerry Davis & Robert Holmes *19 April*	1–4 (All) 625-line PAL 2" VT colour	**October 1983** edited compilation **April 1999**	Same as TV title Terrance Dicks *May 1976*	**Video disc released 1985**
Terror of the Zygons Robert Banks Stewart *30 August*	1–4 (All) 625-line PAL 2" VT colour	**November 1988** omnibus **June 1999**	The Loch Ness Monster Terrance Dicks *January 1976*	**Laser disc pressing April 1998**
Planet of Evil Louis Marks *27 September*	1–4 (All) 625-line PAL 2" VT colour	**January 1994**	Same as TV title Terrance Dicks *August 1977*	**Audio** Incidental music available on compilation CD
Pyramid of Mars Stephen Harris (Lewis Griefer & Robert Holmes) *25 October*	1–4 (All) 625-line PAL 2" VT colour	**February 1985** edited compilation **January 1994**	Same as TV title Terrance Dicks *December 1976*	**Audio** Incidental music available on compilation CD
The Android Invasion Terry Nation *22 November*	1–4 (All) 625-line PAL 2" VT colour	**March 1995**	Same as TV title Terrance Dicks *November 1978*	
1976				
The Brain of Morbius Robin Bland (Terrance Dicks & Robert Holmes) *3 January*	1–4 (All) 625-line PAL 2" VT colour	**July 1984** compilation **July 1990**	Same as TV title Terrance Dicks *June 1977*	**Video disc released 1985** **Audio** Incidental music on compilation CD
The Seeds of Doom Robert Banks Stewart & Robert Holmes *31 January*	1–6 (All) 625-line PAL 2" VT colour	**August 1994** 2 cassettes	Same as TV title Philip Hinchcliffe *February 1977*	
The Masque of Mandragora Louis Marks *4 September*	1–4 (All) 625-line PAL 2" VT colour	**August 1991**	Same as TV title Philip Hinchcliffe *December 1977*	
The Hand of Fear Bob Baker & Dave Martin *2 October*	1–4 (All) 625-line PAL 2" VT colour	**February 1996**	Same as TV title Terrance Dicks *January 1979*	

Story title Writers *UK premiered*	Surviving episodes Media	BBC video released	Novel title Author *First published*	Other media
The Deadly Assassin Robert Holmes *30 October*	1–4 (All) 625-line PAL 2" VT colour	October 1991	Same as TV title Terrance Dicks *October 1977*	

1977

The Face of Evil Chris Boucher *1 January*	1–4 (All) 625-line PAL 2" VT colour	May 1999	Same as TV title Terrance Dicks *January 1978*	
The Robots of Death Chris Boucher *29 January*	1–4 (All) 625-line PAL 2" VT colour	April 1986 edited omnibus February 1995	Same as TV title Terrance Dicks *May 1979*	
The Talons of Weng-Chiang Robert Holmes *26 February*	1–6 (All) 625-line PAL 2" VT colour	November 1988 omnibus – minor edits August 1999	Same as TV title Terrance Dicks *November 1977*	Script Book (Titan Nov 89)
Horror of Fang Rock Terrance Dicks *3 September*	1–4 (All) 625-line PAL 2" VT colour	July 1998	Same as TV title Terrance Dicks *March 1978*	
The Invisible Enemy Bob Baker & Dave Martin *1 October*	1–4 (All) 625-line PAL 2" VT colour		Same as TV title Terrance Dicks *March 1979*	
Image of the Fendahl Chris Boucher *29 October*	1–4 (All) 625-line PAL 2" VT colour	March 1993	Same as TV title Terrance Dicks *July 1979*	
The Sun Makers Robert Holmes *26 November*	1–4 (All) 625-line PAL 2" VT colour		Same as TV title Terrance Dicks *November 1982*	

1978

Underworld Bob Baker & Dave Martin *7 January*	1–4 (All) 625-line PAL 2" VT colour		Same as TV title Terrance Dicks *January 1980*	
The Invasion of Time David Agnew (David Weir, Anthony Read, Graham Williams) *4 February*	1–6 (All) 625-line PAL 2" VT colour		Same as TV title Terrance Dicks *February 1980*	
The Ribos Operation Robert Holmes *2 September*	1–4 (All) 625-line PAL 2" VT colour	April 1995	Same as TV title Ian Marter *December 1979*	
The Pirate Planet Douglas Adams & Anthony Read *30 September*	1–4 (All) 625-line PAL 2" VT colour	April 1995		
The Stones of Blood David Fisher *28 October*	1–4 (All) 625-line PAL 2" VT colour	May 1995	Same as TV title Terrance Dicks *March 1980*	
The Androids of Tara David Fisher *25 November*	1–4 (All) 625-line PAL 2" VT colour	May 1995	Same as TV title Terrance Dicks *April 1980*	
The Power of Kroll Robert Holmes *23 December*	1–4 (All) 625-line PAL 2" VT colour	June 1995	Same as TV title Terrance Dicks *May 1980*	

Story title Writers *UK premiered*	Surviving episodes Media	BBC video released	Novel title Author *First published*	Other media
1979				
The Armageddon Factor Bob Baker & Dave Martin *20 January*	1–6 (All) 625-line PAL 2" VT colour	**June 1995**	**Same as TV title** Terrance Dicks *June 1980*	
Destiny of the Daleks Terry Nation *1 September*	1–4 (All) 625-line PAL 2" VT colour	**July 1994**	**Same as TV title** Terrance Dicks *November 1979*	
City of Death David Agnew (Douglas Adams, Graham Williams & David Fisher) *29 September*	1–4 (All) 625-line PAL 2" VT colour	**April 1991**		
The Creature from the Pit David Fisher *27 October*	1–4 (All) 625-line PAL 2" VT colour		**Same as TV title** David Fisher *January 1981*	
Nightmare of Eden Bob Baker *24 November*	1–4 (All) 625-line PAL 2" VT colour	**January 1999**	**Same as TV title** Terrance Dicks *September 1980*	
The Horns of Nimon Anthony Read *22 December*	1–4 (All) 625-line PAL 2" VT colour		**Same as TV title** Terrance Dicks *October 1980*	
1980				
Shada Douglas Adams *(untransmitted)*	625-line PAL 2" VT colour from 1st studio & all 16mm colour location film	**July 1992** Footage edited with linking material & script		
The Leisure Hive David Fisher *30 August*	1–4 (All) 625-line PAL 2" VT colour	**January 1997**	**Same as TV title** David Fisher *July 1982*	**Audio** Incidental music available on compilation CD
Meglos Andrew McCullough & John Flanagan *27 September*	1–4 (All) 625-line PAL 2" VT colour		**Same as TV title** Terrance Dicks *February 1983*	**Audio** Incidental music available on compilation CD
Full Circle Andrew Smith *25 October*	1–4 (All) 625-line PAL 2" VT colour	**October 1997** *E-Space boxed set*	**Same as TV title** Andrew Smith *September 1982*	**Viewmaster reels** 1981
State of Decay Terrance Dicks *22 November*	1–4 (All) 625-line PAL 2" VT colour	**October 1997** *E-Space boxed sets*	**Same as TV title** Terrance Dicks *September 1981*	**Audio** Pickwick Talking Book 1981
1981				
Warriors' Gate Stephen Gallagher *3 January*	1–4 (All) 625-line PAL 2" VT colour	**October 1997** *E-Space boxed set*	**Same as TV title** John Lydecker (Steve Gallagher) *April 1982*	**Audio** Incidental music available on compilation CD
The Keeper of Traken Johnny Byrne *31 January*	1–4 (All) 625-line PAL 2" VT colour	**June 1993**	**Same as TV title** Terrance Dicks *May 1982*	**Audio** Incidental music available on compilation CD

Story title Writers *UK premiered*	Surviving episodes Media	BBC video released	Novel title Author *First published*	Other media
Logopolis Christopher H. Bidmead *28 February*	1–4 (All) 625-line PAL 2" VT colour	March 1992	Same as TV title Christopher H. Bidmead *October 1982*	
K-9 & Company: A Girl's Best Friend Terence Dudley *28 December*	50 minute pilot (All) 625-line PAL 2" VT colour	August 1995 full pilot version	Same as TV title Terence Dudley *May 1987*	**Audio** Single of theme music 1981

1982

Castrovalva Christopher H. Bidmead *4 January*	1–4 (All) 625-line PAL 2" VT colour	March 1992	Same as TV title Christopher Bidmead *March 1983*	**Audio** Incidental music cassette issued 1983 Viewmaster reels 1982
Four to Doomsday Terence Dudley *18 January*	1–4 (All) 625-line PAL 2" VT colour		Same as TV title Terrance Dicks *April 1983*	**Audio** Incidental music available on compilation CD
Kinda Christopher Bailey *1 February*	1–4 (All) 625-line PAL 2" VT colour	October 1994	Same as TV title Terrance Dicks *December 1983*	**Audio** BBC Talking Book 1996 Incidental music available on compilation CD
The Visitation Eric Saward *15 February*	1–4 (All) 625-line PAL 2" VT colour	July 1994 2 cassettes with *Black Orchid*	Same as TV title Eric Saward *August 1982*	**Making of . . .** Book 1982
Black Orchid Terence Dudley *1 March*	1–2 (All) 625-line PAL 2" VT colour	July 1994 2 cassettes with *The Visitation*	Same as TV title Terence Dudley *September 1986*	
Earthshock Eric Saward *8 March*	1–4 (All) 625-line PAL 2" VT colour	September 1992	Same as TV title Ian Marter *May 1983*	**Audio** Incidental music available on compilation CD
Time-Flight Peter Grimwade *23 March*	1–4 (All) 625-line PAL 2" VT colour		Same as TV title Peter Grimwade *January 1983*	

1983

Arc of Infinity Johnny Byrne *3 January*	1–4 (All) 625-line PAL 2" VT colour	February 1994	Same as TV title Terrance Dicks *July 1983*	**Audio** Incidental music available on compilation CD
Snakedance Christopher Bailey *18 January*	1–4 (All) 625-line PAL 2" VT colour	December 1994	Same as TV title Terrance Dicks *January 1984*	**Audio** Incidental music available on compilation CD
Mawdryn Undead Peter Grimwade *1 February*	1–4 (All) 625-line PAL 2" VT colour	November 1992	Same as TV title Peter Grimwade *August 1983*	**Audio** Incidental music cassette issued 1993

Story title Writers *UK premiered*	Surviving episodes Media	BBC video released	Novel title Author *First published*	Other media
Terminus Steve Gallagher *15 February*	**1–4 (All)** 625-line PAL 2" VT colour	**January 1993**	**Same as TV title** John Lydecker (Steve Gallagher) *June 1983*	
Enlightenment Barbara Clegg *1 March*	**1–4 (All)** 625-line PAL 2" VT colour	**February 1993**	**Same as TV title** Barbara Clegg *February 1984*	**Audio** Incidental music available on compilation CD
The King's Demons Terence Dudley *15 March*	**1–2 (All)** 625-line PAL 2" VT colour	**November 1995** Boxed with *The Five Doctors* special edition & booklet	**Same as TV title** Terence Dudley *February 1986*	**Audio** Incidental music available on compilation CD
The Five Doctors Terrance Dicks *25 November*	**90 minute TV movie (All)** 625-line PAL 2" VT colour & 4 episode version & extended length BBC Video release	**September 1985** edited movie version **July 1990** uncut **November 1995** special edition, boxed with *The King's Demons* & booklet	**Same as TV title** Terrance Dicks *November 1983*	**Laser disc pressings 1985, 1996** **Audio** Incidental music available on compilation CD

1984

Warriors of the Deep Johnny Byrne *5 January*	**1–4 (All)** 625-line PAL 1" VT colour	**September 1995**	**Same as TV title** Terrance Dicks *May 1984*	**Audio** BBC Talking Book 1996 Incidental music available on compilation CD
The Awakening Eric Pringle *19 January*	**1–2 (All)** 625-line PAL 1" VT colour	**March 1997** 2 cassettes with *Frontios*	**Same as TV title** Eric Pringle *February 1985*	**Audio** Incidental music available on compilation CD
Frontios Christopher H. Bidmead *26 January*	**1–4 (All)** 625-line PAL 1" VT colour	**March 1997** 2 cassettes with *The Awakening*	**Same as TV title** Christopher H. Bidmead *September 1984*	
Resurrection of the Daleks Eric Saward *8 February*	**1–2 (All)** 625-line PAL 1" VT colour & 4 episode version	**November 1993**		**Audio** Incidental music available on compilation CD
Planet of Fire Peter Grimwade *23 February*	**1–4 (All)** 625-line PAL 1" VT colour	**September 1998**	**Same as TV title** Peter Grimwade *October 1984*	**Audio** Incidental music available on compilation CD
The Caves of Androzani Robert Holmes *8 March*	**1–4 (All)** 625-line PAL 1" VT colour	**January 1992**	**Same as TV title** Terrance Dicks *November 1984*	**Audio** Incidental music available on compilation CD
The Twin Dilemma Anthony Steven & Eric Saward *22 March*	**1–4 (All)** 625-line PAL 1" VT colour	**May 1992**	**Same as TV title** Eric Saward *October 1985*	

1985

Attack of the Cybermen Paula Moore (Eric Saward & Ian Levine) *5 January*	**1–2 (All)** 625-line PAL 1" VT colour & 4 episode version		**Same as TV title** Eric Saward *April 1989*	**Audio** BBC Talking Book 1996

Story title Writers *UK premiered*	Surviving episodes Media	BBC video released	Novel title Author *First published*	Other media
Vengeance on Varos Philip Martin *19 January*	1–2 (All) 625-line PAL I" VT colour & 4 episode version	**May 1993**	**Same as TV title** Philip Martin *January 1988*	**Audio** BBC Talking Book 1997
The Mark of the Rani Pip & Jane Baker *2 February*	1–2 (All) 625-line PAL I" VT colour & 4 episode version	**July 1995**	**Same as TV title** Pip & Jane Baker *January 1986*	
The Two Doctors Robert Holmes *16 February*	1–3 (All) 625-line PAL I" VT colour & 6 episode version	**November 1993**	**Same as TV title** Robert Holmes *August 1985*	
Timelash Glen McCoy *9 March*	1–2 (All) 625-line PAL I" VT colour & 4 episode version	**January 1998**	**Same as TV title** Glen McCoy *December 1985*	**Audio** Incidental music available on compilation CD
Revelation of the Daleks Eric Saward *23 March*	1–2 (All) 625-line PAL I" VT colour & 4 episode version			
Radio serial: Slipback Eric Saward *25 July*	1–6 (All) BBC digital audio recording		**Same as radio play title** Eric Saward *August 1986*	**Audio** BBC Audio Collection (Nov 97)

1986

The Trial of a Time Lord (1–4) *(aka The Mysterious Planet)* Robert Holmes *6 September*	1–4 (All) 625-line PAL I" VT colour	**October 1993** all 14 episodes in 30th anniversary TARDIS tin packaging	**The Mysterious Planet** Terrance Dicks *November 1987*	
The Trial of a Time Lord (5–8) *(aka Mindwarp)* Philip Martin *4 October*	1–4 (All) 625-line PAL I" VT colour	**October 1993** all 14 episodes in 30th anniversary TARDIS tin packaging	**Mindwarp** Philip Martin *June 1989*	
The Trial of a Time Lord (9–12) *(aka Terror of the Vervoids)* Pip & Jane Baker *1 November*	1–4 (All) 625-line PAL I" VT colour	**October 1993** all 14 episodes in 30th anniversary TARDIS tin packaging	**Terror of the Vervoids** Pip & Jane Baker *September 1987*	
The Trial of a Time Lord (13–14) *(aka The Ultimate Foe)* Robert Holmes, Pip & Jane Baker *29 November*	1–2 (All) 625-line PAL I" VT colour	**October 1993** all 14 episodes in 30th anniversary TARDIS tin packaging	**The Ultimate Foe** Pip & Jane Baker *April 1988*	

1987

Time and the Rani Pip & Jane Baker *7 September*	1–4 (All) 625-line PAL I" VT colour	**July 1995**	**Same as TV title** Pip & Jane Baker *December 1987*	
Paradise Towers Stephen Wyatt *5 October*	1–4 (All) 625-line PAL I" VT colour	**October 1995**	**Same as TV title** Stephen Wyatt *December 1988*	
Delta and the Bannermen Malcolm Kohl *2 November*	1–3 (All) 625-line PAL I" VT colour		**Same as TV title** Malcolm Kohl *January 1989*	
Dragonfire Ian Briggs *23 November*	1–3 (All) 625-line PAL I" VT colour	**January 1994**	**Same as TV title** Ian Briggs *March 1989*	

Story title Writers *UK premiered*	Surviving episodes Media	BBC video released	Novel title Author *First published*	Other media
1988				
Remembrance of the Daleks Ben Aaronovitch *15 October*	1–4 (All) 625-line PAL 1" VT colour	September 1993 episodes in 30th anniversary commemorative tin & booklet	Same as TV title Ben Aaronovitch *June 1990*	
The Happiness Patrol Graeme Curry *2 November*	1–3 (All) 625-line PAL 1" VT colour	August 1997	Same as TV title Graeme Curry *February 1990*	
Silver Nemesis Kevin Clarke *23 November*	1–3 (All) 625-line PAL 1" VT colour & extended BBC Video release	April 1993 extended length episodes	Same as TV title Kevin Clarke *November 1989*	**Making of . . .** Documentary by PBS television of USA 1988
The Greatest Show in the Galaxy Stephen Wyatt *14 December*	1–4 (All) 625-line PAL 1" VT colour	July 1999	Same as TV title Stephen Wyatt *December 1989*	
1989				
Battlefield Ben Aaronovitch *6 September*	1–4 (All) 625-line PAL 1" VT colour	March 1998	Same as TV title Marc Platt *July 1991*	
Ghost Light Marc Platt *4 October*	1–3 (All) 625-line PAL 1" VT colour	April 1994	Same as TV title Marc Platt *September 1990*	**Script Book** (Titan Jun 1993)
The Curse of Fenric Ian Briggs *25 October*	1–4 (All) 625-line PAL 1" VT colour	February 1991 extended length episodes	Same as TV title Ian Briggs *November 1990*	**Audio** Incidental music available on CD
Survival Rona Munro *22 November*	1–3 (All) 625-line PAL 1" VT colour	October 1995	Same as TV title Rona Munro *September 1990*	
1993				
Radio serial: The Paradise of Death Barry Letts *27 August*	1–5 (All) BBC digital audio recording		Same as radio title Barry Letts *April 1994*	**Audio** BBC Audio Collection (1993)
1996				
Radio serial: The Ghosts of N-Space Barry Letts *20 January*	1–6 (All) BBC digital audio recording		Same as radio title Barry Letts *March 1995*	**Audio** BBC Audio Collection (1996)
Doctor Who – The Movie *(aka The Enemy Within)* Matthew Jacobs *27 May*	90 minute TV movie 525-line 1" colour	May 1996 US TV movie version	Doctor Who Gary Russell *May 1996*	**Audio** BBC Talking Book (1997) Incidental music available on promo CD **Making of . . .** Book 'Regeneration' Gary Russell & Philip Segal (Virgin 1999)

© Jeremy Bentham, March 1999

ACKNOWLEDGEMENTS

I am especially grateful to Jeremy Bentham for supplying photographs from his own extensive collection as well as for compiling the invaluable Preservation Archive. Among those other people whose help and co-operation in the past as well as during the actual writing of this book I wish to acknowledge are: the late Heather Hartnell, Sydney Newman, Terry Nation, Patrick Troughton, Jon Pertwee, Peter Cushing and Robert Holmes; plus Verity Lambert, Ray Cusick, Barry Letts, Tom Baker, John Nathan-Turner, Peter Davison, Tony Harding, Colin Baker, Sylvester McCoy and Paul McGann. Thanks, lastly but not least, to Heather Holden-Brown at Headline who instigated the project, and my two delightful editors Lorraine Jerram and Nuala Buffini.

Peter Haining

PHOTOGRAPH CREDITS

Tom Baker: 92

BBC: 3, 8, 10, 29t, 59, 65, 69, 73, 74, 80, 85, 91, 95, 97, 99, 101, 111, 113, 114, 117, 118, 121, 133, 135, 147, 149, 151, 152, 157, 158, 159, 164, 166, 169, 173, 175

BBC Worldwide: 18, 21, 22, 64

Jeremy Bentham Collection: 11, 55, 79, 83, 89, 98, 104, 110

Phil Bevan: 51

Ray Cusick: 27, 32-3, 53

Daily Mail: 106

Express Features: 87

Peter Haining Collection: 15, 29b, 37, 109

Heather Hartnell: 23

National Film Archive: 9, 38, 41, 44, 45, 48-9

Stephen Payne: 145

Rex Features: 163

Solo Syndication: 129, 130, 139, 141

Thames Television: 125

Patrick Troughton: 56, 63

Colour Section Page 1. Peter Haining Collection; **2.** Peter Haining Collection (t) and Ronald Grant Archive (b); **3.** BBC; **4.** Jeremy Bentham Collection (t) and BBC (b); **5.** BBC; **6.** Jeremy Bentham Collection; **7.** Solo Syndication (t) and BBC (b); **8.** BBC.